FAMOUS LANDMARKS

A NOVEL

ROB BECK

TYBALT BOOKS

ISBN: 979-8-9988513-0-8

1

JUNE 2005

"Which one of us gets the bedroom?" Eugene asked, standing in the living room of a sublet in San Francisco.

"You take it," Adam said. "I like the living room."

"So, is all this working for you fellas?" Darren said. He was a friend of Adam's older brother, Joel, showing them the place and explaining about the trash and laundry. Their first grown-up apartment. They didn't need to figure out who'd take which room because they never went after the same thing. That was especially true when they were checking out the guys.

And they attracted different types of guys, too. Boys who favored short and compact like a gymnast preferred Adam Silverman. The ones who wanted a tall swimmer chose Eugene Cho.

Darren told them which way to walk if they wanted to see that famous row of houses in Alamo Square. The apartment was also pretty close to the Panhandle, whatever that was. They got the rundown on grocery and hardware stores too, and Eugene, who was a fitness trainer, had already researched the gym.

But in any case, they had already committed, on the

strength of Joel's good word and a few emails and phone calls, to take the sublet, and were ready to like it, whatever it was. And it was better than they could've imagined. The furniture was nothing fancy, but Darren must've been making bank to live in an apartment like that alone.

"I think I could live here for a while," said Adam, grinning.

"Me too."

The Brooklynites looked at each other. They were really living in San Francisco—at least through the end of September. Move-in would be several days later, after Darren had pushed off for Asia.

After settling up with Darren and thanking him, they walked out into the sunshine stunned but ready for adventure. They weren't in any hurry to get back to their hostel west of Union Square, which was filled with European tourists who smoked cigarettes in the stairways, setting off the alarm at all hours. They were supposed to go to a party the next night on Dolores Street hosted by Evan Bronstein, another homo dude a couple of years ahead of them in school. But for the moment, they were free.

So they wandered, checking out the new world around them, not caring where they were going. The found the Panhandle, which turned out to be a park, and when they got to the Haight-Ashbury neighborhood, the sidewalk rose steeply in front of them. The houses were some of the most beautiful they had ever seen, as grand as anything in Brooklyn Heights or Manhattan but different—brighter, more colorful, more fanciful. Some of them were nicely painted and well-kept, but there were shabby ones and ugly ones too. It didn't matter—everything was waiting to be explored. Soon the boys found themselves on a curving ramp of a road circling Buena Vista Park. The streets to their left dropped away at a seemingly impossible angle.

"Man, I feel like we could fall off!" said Eugene.

The city spread below them in thousands of houses all the way down to San Francisco Bay. The hills on the other side of the water shimmered, veiled by the atmosphere, melting into the clouds.

Gradually, they made a labyrinthian descent and found themselves on Castro Street. The old movie theater sign was visible in the distance with residential buildings stacked up on the hill beyond it like presents among the trees.

"I bet we could find a drink down there," said Adam.

"And something to eat," said Eugene.

"That's the gayborhood, right?"

"Yup."

The next evening, they were getting ready for Evan Bronstein's party. Adam rummaged through a big duffel, unpacking stacks of clothes. "I have no idea what the hell to wear." He held a purple tie-dyed T-shirt up to his chest. "How about this? It's kind of San Francisco."

"It'll get cold after sundown," Eugene said.

"Good point. I guess I'll take a hoodie too."

Eugene put on a grey-blue thermal that showed off his broad shoulders and olive skin. Dudes melted when they met Eugene.

When they were dressed to go, they studied the transit map and figured out the train that brought them from the airport was a different system from the one that served most of the city.

"Is it okay to bore tunnels in earthquake country?" Adam wondered.

They decided the simplest way to get there would be to walk the short distance to Market Street and get the J Church, and were surprised when the J emerged from the Metro tunnel and rolled along the street. They figured out that it must be a streetcar, which was different from a cable car. The whole thing was confusing.

Evan lived in a flat on Dolores with two other guys. Between the three roommates, they knew a lot of people. Adam and Eugene arrived to a well-attended sausage fest, mostly yuppie types. Everybody was under thirty-five. The apartment was sparse and tasteful with track lighting and beige walls and black and white photos. It didn't exactly seem lived in.

Adam said to Eugene, "I feel like I'm in the wrong tax bracket."

Some friendly nerd greeted them and they explained they were Evan's friends from New York. That produced Evan from the beige depths of the apartment.

"Hey guys! I can't believe you're here!"

He hugged them too hard. He asked them what they were doing, which, until lately, hadn't been much except finishing up school, working and saving money, then spending it on this trip. Evan mentioned his tech job, told them again how glad he was to see them, and then disappeared.

Adam and Eugene decided to check out the beverage options. On a table in the living room, there were bottles of questionable wine and a few standard brands of spirits and stuff to mix with them. The ice was almost out.

"I dunno—red wine?" Adam didn't sound too excited.

"Yeah, sure," said Eugene, equally unenthusiastic. They poured some into plastic cups and sipped. Eugene made a "could be worse" face. Adam concurred.

They went over to some boys standing around the food. A pretty little sparrow of a guy only slightly taller than Adam was telling about how he made the hummus. Easy on the eyes, boring. Adam and Eugene moved on.

In a room toward the back, a very tall, lanky dude with wavy, dark blond hair, wearing a leather jacket over a white Oxford button-down, was standing by a wall, telling some dippy boys all about the testing of the hydrogen bomb. He was good looking in a '70s porn kind of way and was clearly at least one sheet to the wind. His audience seemed to be really into what he was talking about. There may have been some bullshit in that bomb for all anyone could tell, but the delivery was entertaining. He noticed Adam and Eugene and gave them the eye. A perv.

They wandered into the adjacent room, which turned out to be the kitchen, and to their relief, they found beer. Nobody knew it was there, but two guys had discovered it and were helping themselves from the fridge. Adam and Eugene abandoned their half-glasses of wine and popped a couple of brews before they stepped through a door leading to the back stairs and a small wooden deck.

"Whaddya think?" asked Eugene, looking into the twilight.

"These guys are a bunch of clowns," Adam said, "but the one talking about the bomb is hot in a sleazy way. He's got some brains, too."

"He was definitely checking us out."

"Yeah. I'll bet he's a garbage dick, but sometimes those guys are fun."

Eugene suggested that if either of them saw an opportunity, he should go for it.

"Works for me," said Adam, "but we'll see."

They went back inside. Interest in the bomb lecture had started to drift a little. One of the boys stretched and complained his shoulders were tight. He was flighty but cute.

Eugene, whose lean, supple musculature could've broken him in half, said in his innocent way, "I might be able to relieve that a little, if you wouldn't mind me touching you."

Adam smiled to himself as he watched Eugene come on so harmless at first.

"You're smiling. You must be enjoying yourself." It was the tall perv talking to Adam.

"I guess I must be. My name's Adam."

"Pleased to meet you, Adam. I'm Randall. I'm a friend of Tim's."

"I'm a friend of Evan's from college. Me and my buddy Eugene, the guy giving the massage, are visiting from Brooklyn for the summer."

"Welcome to San Francisco. I wouldn't want to impose, but should you so desire, I would be glad to show you some of the sights." It didn't exactly sound like a pickup line, but he was definitely into Adam.

Eugene had started to attract attention. He lured another willing victim into his crushing grip. The guy was moaning.

"Your friend seems to know what he's doing. He's quite the sadist," Randall said, evidently impressed.

"Eugene could get rich doing that to people, but he's a personal trainer."

"And may I ask what you do?"

"I haven't figured that out yet. I just graduated from college this spring. I'm on a little vacation before I think about it seriously, though I should get a job here so I'm not living on black coffee."

"I believe there's a temp position open in the MFA office at the College of the Urban Environment. I'm a student there."

"Thanks for the tip," Adam said. "I'll check that out. So what are you studying?"

Randall said that at the moment he was taking a summer seminar, Literature of the Counterculture. He went on about the Beat Generation, the Merry Pranksters, and the San Francisco Sound. Some of the things he mentioned Adam knew and was able to talk about them a little. He also learned Randall was a photographer, liked old Leicas, and made his living working for a photo supply and film processing company. He surfed at Ocean Beach. While Randall geeked out, Adam watched the way his throat moved and his intelligent hands. An odd guy but sexy.

"Would you care to step out onto the deck with me?" Randall asked. "I'd just like to get a little fresh air."

By then, the sky had darkened, and the fog had come in. Lights were on in the houses on the other side of the garden fence. A couple of other guests were standing on the deck talking, but the weather had cooled off and they started moving inside.

"San Francisco is chillier than Brooklyn in June," said Adam.

"Are you cold?" asked Randall. "We can go back in."

"I'm okay for now. It's actually nice compared to the mugginess I'm used to." Adam put his hands on the wooden rail, resting his weight in front of him, and looked into the deep blue twilight made opaque by the cloud cover. Randall stood next to him and leaned against the rail too. Adam said, "I've always thought this city would be interesting, but somehow I never thought about coming here until my brother told me about this sublet I lucked into."

"How long are you here for?"

"Through the end of September."

"Do you know what you're doing after that?"

"No, I don't. But I'm not gonna think about it tonight at my very first party in Frisco."

"Pardon me, but we call it San Francisco here."

"Oops—sorry," Adam said with a laugh. "It's my first party in San Francisco, and I've already said the wrong thing."

"Just for that, we may have to spank you."

"Oh yeah? I always heard you people over here were kinky."

"If you stick around long enough, you might just find out." Randall brushed against Adam. They were almost elbow to elbow, leaning on the rail.

"I might at that," said Adam, nudging back and grinning.

"You're really cute," said Randall. A perv on the make.

"Oh yeah?" Adam said, looking at Randall sidelong.

Randall went in for a kiss.

When they came up for air, Adam stepped away from the edge of the deck, moving against the wall of the house where it was a little darker. "Let's go over here." Randall came closer and put his hands around Adam's waist. Adam stood on tiptoe. "I might need a stepladder for this."

After a while, Randall said, "I can tell you're getting cold. Shall we go somewhere more private?"

"Well, normally I would, and I don't object to sex before the first date, but I've had a ton of new stuff to get used to these last couple of days. I think I need to go back to my room and have a little quiet. How about we get together some other time?"

"I'd like that very much. Are you sure you won't be cold and lonely by yourself on this chilly, foggy night?"

"Nah. I've got Eugene to keep me warm."

"How cozy."

"Hey, what are friends for?"

"Before we do some snuggling of our own, would you like to have dinner?"

"Yeah, sure. We could even wear clothes."

"Maybe in the restaurant."

2

JASON FOWLER, soft and puppyish, wearing his office clothes minus the shoes, stood in the kitchen he and Gustavo Cortez shared with two other young men in an upper story Potrero Hill flat. He poured boiling water into a mug, then carried it into the bedroom and put it down on the night table next to the lump under the comforter. The sun lit the wall above. Gustavo slowly poked his head out from the covers as if tasting the air like a snake, a sexy snake with soft, straight, longish hair. "Mmmm... tea. Thank you, baby."

Jason frowned. "I wish I could get back in bed and snuggle."

"I should get up and get ready for class," Gustavo murmured, eyes closed. He made no effort to move.

"Do you want me to come by the store when you're done tonight?" Jason asked. "We could get some food."

"Yeah, that would be good."

Jason and Gustavo had been living together for three months. They had met because Gustavo knew some guys with a regular weekly video art project at a South of Market bar, and he had turned up to check it out on a night when Jason was there having a few drinks, taking a stab at adulthood. Gustavo liked Jason's plump, round cheeks in front and in back. Jason blushed prettily at the attention, hanging on every word. He had come from Orange County to try to make his way in San Francisco, hoping to break away from his life somehow. Whatever that meant, it probably didn't have anything to do with the tech job he thought himself lucky to have but didn't really value.

Gustavo was a San Francisco native. At twenty-three, he had already spent a year traveling, supporting himself along the way, writing and meeting people. For the moment, he was working in Lacey's bookstore and taking classes at the College of the Urban Environment. He was also spooning with Jason, who was sweet and gentle.

As Jason got ready to leave for the office, he watched for a moment as Gustavo forgot about his tea, the pile of books on the floor, the rumpled jeans, the messenger bag, and a summer seminar on the Literature of the Counterculture for a little while longer. He'd probably pull on the jeans at the last minute, suck down the lukewarm tea, and walk out the door without having showered, still somehow smelling good.

A few blocks away, Adam got out of a bus looking more groomed than usual in chinos and a button-down shirt, struggling to get his bearings in the midmorning light. In a little while, he was walking through the door of the main building of the College for the Urban Environment. He followed a sign down a corridor to the Master of Fine Arts office.

"Hi, my name is Adam Silverman. I have a nine thirty appointment with Ted Schacter." A woman with wavy grey hair and a batik scarf at the front desk directed Adam to an inner room. Ted was tall, mid-fifties and fit, with a warm, attractive, lived-in face. He stood to shake Adam's hand.

"Good to meet you. I'm Ted. I'm glad you found this office.

Sometimes I wonder how I found it too. This is only my first year as director of this program since they kidnapped me from the Department of Critical Studies. Anyway, please sit. So, you're in San Francisco for the summer?"

"Yeah, I wanted to take a little time after graduation to do something I'd never done before, and my brother's friend was looking for someone to sublet his apartment."

"You're at a wonderful age to do something like that," Ted said with a smile. "And I see you're a New Yorker. I can hear it too—your accent's a little like mine. Don't hold this against me but I'm from New Jersey. I grew up in Paramus, which I left in the '70s, first for a short stop in New York, then here."

"I can see why you decided to come to San Francisco," said Adam. "If this is what the summer weather is like, I can already tell I'm gonna have a hard time going back."

Ted grinned. "You're not the first person to say that. Anyway, lemme tell you a little about the job. It's a fixed-term position through the end of August, though we might be able to add a few weeks if you're interested. You'd be helping us with data mining, digitizing old records, and getting some reports together. It's part of a college-wide assessment we've been asked to do. Lately, we've seen a trend of declining enrollments. You probably already know the humanities are struggling a bit at the moment. Can I get you a cup of coffee? No? I've been drinking way too much coffee since I took over as director of this program. Lots of long days, not that you'd be asked to put in those kinds of hours. I know you're in San Francisco to have fun. Anyway, the college opened in 1969. The wanted to call it the College for Urban Life until someone pointed out that 'C-U-L' is the French word for tush. They added the MFA program in 1978. Since it's the summer, things are quieter though we have a few courses and there's a seminar series that faculty across the humanities departments participate in. But let me

introduce you to Delma, our office manager, and I can get
another cup of coffee."

"Their student services manager," Adam explained to Eugene
back at the apartment, "just kind of left under mysterious
circumstances. Extended medical leave. I think Ted was trying
to tell me she went nuts."

"I hope that's not a warning," said Eugene.

"It could be. That was a pretty crazy interview. He just kind
of rambled for a while, then shook my hand and asked if I
could come in tomorrow. And I still don't really know what it's
all about except that I'll be working with a lot of enrollment
data and some patchy old financial records. But it seems okay,
for a temp job, anyway. They're planning to post the manager's
position sometime soon, but they need someone to keep things
running over the summer."

The boys had moved into their new address the day before.
They made Adam a curtain for the living room door out of a
cheap, colorful bedspread they bought on Haight Street, tacking
it to the top of the picture molding. Adam was still trying to figure
out what to do with his clothes, not having thought much about
that when he chose to set himself up in the living room. For the
moment, he had hung some shirts and pants in the hall closet. His
socks and underwear were still in the duffel bag, which meant
trafficking stacks of clothes around till he found what he wanted.

Eugene leaned in the doorway, watching Adam get ready
for a date with Randall.

"You could just leave all that stuff on the coffee table or
something."

"I thought about that, but it might be as obnoxious as living
out of the bag."

Eugene thought maybe he had found work too. "I put in an

application at the gym. The guy at the front counter said they were looking for trainers but didn't bother introducing me to anyone. I dunno. Maybe it'll turn into something."

"They'd be stupid not to interview you." Adam headed for the hall closet. Eugene watched him pull out a black and dark red bowling shirt from his limited travel wardrobe. "Whaddya think?"

"That should be good," said Eugene. "You said he has a beatnik thing, right?"

"Yeah. He's interested in Beats and hippies and the San Francisco Renaissance and a ton of other stuff. Smart guy. A little intense."

"But you like weirdos."

"Yeah, I do," said Adam. "And he's got a hot mouth."

Randall was waiting for Adam outside a sushi place in a busy restaurant row. Longtime residents of the neighborhood plodded among the hipsters, yuppies and assorted freaks choking the sidewalk. As Adam approached, Randall's glazed-over resting face turned into a smile.

"You made it. I think you'll really like this place. How did you get here?"

"I took a bus, then walked part of the way," said Adam. "I'm not sure I have the hang of the buses yet." Adam noticed some guys wearing cowboy outfits and carrying a guitar, a fiddle, and a trumpet. "Hey, are those mariachis?"

"Yeah. They often play in the Mexican restaurants around here. We should go to one sometime."

"Is this the Mission?"

"Good question," said Randall. "Let's go inside."

When they were seated, Randall suggested they order some sake.

"Hm—looks like there's a hot one and a couple of cold ones," said Adam.

"I believe the more complex ones are served cold."

"Let's get a cold one."

Randall ordered the sake from one of the servers while Adam puzzled over the names of the menu items. The server said she'd come back.

"Is one of these things blowfish?" Adam asked.

"You mean fugu. It's considered a delicacy in Japan but contains a neurotoxin that causes paralysis. You can die of asphyxiation because your muscles shut down so you stop breathing. A very slight dose supposedly produces a tingling sensation in the lips, though it would have to be really slight. Any amount could easily kill you."

"Maybe we don't order the fugu," said Adam.

"Don't worry—they don't have it here. It would be a lot of extra trouble and probably be pretty expensive too. Even if they did have it, it might be okay because farmed fugu is less poisonous, and they wouldn't serve the most toxic parts of the fish. But it's still possible to make a mistake."

Adam tried to make sense of the sushi and sashimi order form. "I like Japanese food, but I don't know what I'm doing."

"Neither do I, really," said Randall.

" Aw c'mon—you just told me all about fugu."

"I can tell you what will poison you."

"At least I know I won't die. How about a California roll?"

"That will poison *me*," Randall said. "I have a shellfish allergy. But please go ahead, if you want one."

Their sake arrived and they over-ordered dinner.

Adam said, "We should toast my new employment. I followed your tip and got the temp job at CUE in the MFA program."

"Oh, really? May I ask, doing what?"

"I'll be helping them compile data for some kind of department review. It sounds boring, but I like the director."

"Ted Schacter? He's a really smart guy. And from what I can tell, he has the crotch of a donkey."

"I might have noticed something donkey-like there."

"And who wouldn't? Well, congratulations. Here's to your new employment!"

"To my new employment. And to men with donkey crotches."

Just then, music blasted near the front. The buskers they saw earlier had found their way in.

Adam laughed. "The mariachis!"

"I'm not really sure what they're doing in a Japanese restaurant."

"Man—this is awesome!"

If Ted Schacter could've overheard the boys talking about him, he would've been highly amused, especially now that he was a senior faculty administrator. Still in the office at seven twenty-five p.m., he decided he'd worked enough for one day. The current era at CUE was not what he had signed up for. Besides preferring to devote his summers to travel and his own projects, he didn't much love his new role because it came to him in a time of crisis. The previous year, the college president had resigned ahead of an impending financial scandal. The faculty had elected a member of their ranks to take over, and now they were in the middle of a comprehensive internal audit. Some other people had chosen that moment to slink away too, including the former director of the MFA program, a departure which was really for the best.

When Ted had stepped in, he'd had a lot of fires to put out. The joys of teaching about things that gave the human experience its meaning had given way to seemingly endless discussions about growing financial concerns. At the same time, the student services manager in the program, always a little erratic, had gone completely bananas. She'd had two medical absences of several weeks each, then she was out indefinitely. Ted and the office manager, Delma Duarte, were still discovering little disasters in the files all the time. In some cases, an expense hadn't been paid, or someone had been paid for the wrong thing or paid too much. They'd even found an entire drawer full of old to-do lists, and it was anybody's guess what had actually been done.

With input from Delma, Ted was rewriting the description for the vacant position. In the meantime, they had hired a temp to help with the audit and cleanup—a cute, studly little Brooklyn boy fresh out of school who had come to San Francisco to check things out. He seemed like he'd do just fine.

Putting on his sport coat and slinging the shoulder strap of his briefcase over his head, Ted locked up the office and headed for the street, wandering westward toward Valencia. He was thinking about grabbing some takeout, but maybe first he'd visit a bookstore that stayed open late, a stop on the way home which was becoming a weekly habit. A student he knew worked there, Gustavo Cortez, an elfin hippy-punk boy who could write. He had taken a class of Ted's in the fall, and the professor had made a careful point of not concentrating too much on the young man at the time.

Gustavo was at the register ringing up a customer. He saw Ted and smiled. Ted smiled back and waved, then went to look at a sale table. Every author, every dust jacket, every illustration beckoned, mingling the enticing promise of an as-yet unread book with the pleasure of Gustavo's presence. After several minutes of sampling pages at random, he made his choices, then carried his treasures to the counter.

"Ted!" Gustavo's smile made him even sexier.

"How's it goin', Gustavo?"

"Going okay. I'm doing one of the seminars this summer."

"Yeah, I thought I saw you in the building. Which one are you taking?"

"Literature of the Counterculture."

"Nice. How are you enjoying the counterculture?"

"As countercultures go, it's pretty groovy. I've been wanting to read that stuff for a long time."

"Glad to hear that. The seminars are really nice this year."

"Yeah. I didn't expect CUE to offer something juicy like that over the summer. I'd wondered if it would be all remedial math or whatever."

Any student at CUE was going to be in some way nontraditional, and Gustavo was definitely not an average student anywhere. His papers had snap—something that made him even more bewitching to Ted.

Gustavo rang up the sale, and Ted paid in cash.

"Arright," Ted said with a smile. "I gotta get outta here and get some dinner to take home."

"What's for dinner?"

"A burrito, probably."

"Yeah," Gustavo nodded. "I see a burrito in my immediate future too."

Out on the sidewalk with his new books in his briefcase, Ted headed for a taqueria, humming a song about flowers in springtime. There was a transubstantiation to be found in the knowledge that soon someone who made his heart beat faster would be eating a burrito too.

The lights of the Mission glowed golden in the moist evening air as noisy, happy people passed in and out of bars and restaurants. Adam and Randall stood waiting for a cab, Adam holding a paper box full of leftovers.

"I feel bad," Adam said. "I shouldn't have ordered crab."

"Don't feel bad," said Randall. "I did tell you it was okay. And you weren't the idiot who tried to eat some but shouldn't have. Sorry, I didn't mean to suggest that you might be one of two idiots."

Adam laughed. "No offense taken. How're you doing?"

"My mouth and throat are kind of swollen. It was just a taste. I think I caught it in time. Wanna go back to my place?"

"Dude, you just had a shellfish allergy reaction. I don't think we're getting freaky tonight."

"Okay then, come back with me and make sure I don't need to go to the emergency room. If I'm not dead at dawn, I'll drive you home."

"Yeah, sure."

In the dark of the cab, Randall rested his hand on the inside of Adam's thigh. The city sped by outside, made impressionistic by the fog. Adam tried to keep up with every change in the terrain as the car went over crests and valleys, past houses and parks. The Pacific churned in the distance, invisible and at the same time brought nearer by the mist. At last, they pulled up in front of a bland stucco house.

"My place is in the back, behind the garage," Randall explained. He opened a side door and led the way past the washer and dryer to a small studio apartment with a futon on the floor. There were clothes, notebooks, loose sheets of paper, cameras, and other photographic equipment everywhere. Next to the closet was a surfboard. "Sorry about the mess. Here, let me get you a chair."

"Don't worry about me. Go lie down."

Adam went to take a leak, and the bathroom wasn't much tidier. At least the toilet wasn't too bad. When he got back, Randall said, "Hey, I'm really sorry about all this."

"Don't worry about it." Adam yawned. "It was a really interesting evening."

"A little too interesting."

"Well, other than the shellfish thing. I had a good time."

"Me too. Wanna put that sushi in the fridge?"

"Oh yeah, thanks."

Randall put the takeout box in the refrigerator. Adam got down to his t-shirt and undies and stretched out on the futon with his hands behind his head. Randall undressed too and lay down next to him.

Adam said, "I get how it could be considered disrespectful for a visitor to call San Francisco by a nickname. It would be like doing that to a person without being invited."

"An interesting comparison. I hadn't thought of that."

Suddenly Randall laughed. "I probably shouldn't mention this, but one time I was trading insults with a friend in Los Angeles, which I referred to as 'La La Land.' So he called San Francisco 'Sandy Fran.'"

"Ha! That's a good burn."

"Yeah, I thought so, too. Does Brooklyn have any offensive nicknames?"

"Nah, we'd beat people up. Just kidding, though maybe it would depend on who's listening. Anyway, I've never heard anything offensive. You sometimes you see it called the Borough of Churches, but that's an old fashioned name. Nobody says that."

"Yeah, besides, that's nowhere as good as 'Sandy Fran.'"

Adam laughed. "Man, that's really vile."

"Worth beating someone up."

"Or you could just say, 'Pardon me, but we call it San Francisco here.'"

"Very good," Randall grinned. "You catch on fast."

3

SATURDAY MORNING. Oliver Larsen tied his red-gold curls into a ponytail, strapped on a bicycle helmet, and rode out from his parents' house through the early morning Oakland streets to MacArthur BART station, headed for a day at Grateful Peas Grocery across the Bay. The train screeched in the tunnels, making it difficult to read the book about organic farming he brought with him. Once he was on the San Francisco side of the Transbay Tube, he got out a few stops early and pedaled off toward the Mission. The cars were out to kill him.

When he arrived at the store, his coworkers greeted him with no more personality than the blocks of tofu in the refrigerator. The manager was almost completely flat of affect, possibly due to being an android in the shape of a tall, broad, hirsute hipster, and looked right through everyone. But there was Damon who talked about oak leaf lettuce and fresh fava beans. He was handsome too, though the things he said were sometimes hard to understand.

Oliver went upstairs, stashed his stuff in his locker, put on an apron, and clocked in. As jobs went, it wasn't terrible for a short-term option. The time passed quickly. And Grateful Peas was trying to do the right thing. Even if the place was full of yuppies, the store supported local farmers, and Oliver got a discount on groceries. Without the discount, the prices at Grateful Peas were pretty high.

Oliver was headed toward the dairy fridge when his phone buzzed in his pocket. The number belonged to Randall, whom he'd met through Green Rainbow, the queer environmental group he'd been spending time with. Randall was smart and thoughtful and good-looking in a boy-next-door way. The Green Rainbow meeting was on Wednesday evening. Maybe Randall was calling about that. Oliver would pick up the message on his break.

On the other side of the freeway on Potrero Hill, Gustavo was still under the covers, a mystery under an ocean of comforter. Jason slid in next to him and kissed his shoulder with cute little cupid-boy lips. Gustavo murmured contentedly. He rolled over and put his arm around Jason. And then after a while said, "I want churros."

Jason giggled. "We could go out and get some."

"Or doughnuts." Gustavo hugged Jason around the ribs and snuggled against him. "Or we could just stay here and get hungrier while I perv on you."

"That would be good. So would banana pancakes," said Jason.

"Mmmm... nanner cakes. Okay." Gustavo took a noisy breath, rolled out of bed, and found some sweatpants. "Lemme make myself sort of kind of presentable." He wandered down the hall to the bathroom.

Jason went to get socks from the dresser and noticed a flyer for an open mic later that week at the bookstore where Gustavo worked. Gustavo had said he might read something he'd written. Jason didn't write or play an instrument or sing or otherwise make anything.

Gustavo came back with a freshly brushed mouth, looking more awake. He grabbed a hoodie from the closet.

"You okay, Jason? You seem preoccupied or something."

"Just hungry."

"Sorry, baby. I'll put on shoes and we'll go."

In a Market Street gym, Eugene was working with his first client of the day. Steve McGinnis considered himself a basically fit guy, or had been until lately. Maybe he wasn't so fit anymore. A busy life had had unintended consequences.

"I've gone to seed," Steve said with a sigh.

Eugene chuckled. "Well, let's get you back to where you want to be."

Between sets, Eugene found out Steve and his boyfriend Hector were part-owners of an adult video company. Eugene was totally impressed.

"Man—I wanna get paid to film people having sex!"

"And maybe you could," Steve chuckled. "It's a fun business. But it's also a lot of hustle if you want to make a living at it."

Steve had started as an escort. At forty-seven, he was still tying people up for good money, but sooner or later, he'd need to retire from that. So he and Hector worked long hours at the business, where there was too little activity and too much takeout. Hector's own body type was roly-poly, which Steve found sexy, but Hector was also twelve years younger and had a boyish face. Steve was having trouble recognizing himself in the mirror.

"Can we do this without the stationary bike?"

"Totally," said Eugene.

"Good, cause I'd rather turn into a marshmallow than get on that thing."

Eugene was intensely curious about Steve's work.

"So you must see a lot of crazy stuff, huh?"

"Sure, but you get used to it. It's a job. And the guys you meet aren't as wild as they used to be. The city's changed a lot."

"Like how?"

Steve had moved to San Francisco from Florida in the '80s when the plague was at its worst, but even in that grim, terrifying time, a unique mixture of sex, politics and creativity was in the air.

"Folks here don't seem to have as much imagination these days. It's not as interesting."

"That's too bad," said Eugene, clearly disappointed. "That was the sort of thing my buddy and I came here hoping to find."

"Well, maybe it's not like it used to be, but this town still does things to people."

Adam was having a lazy, scruffy Saturday morning, enjoying a little alone time in the apartment when the doorbell rang. It was Randall, wearing his smirk. He held two paper cups.

"Greetings. I brought you coffee."

"Thanks," said Adam, carefully taking the cup. His lip hovered over the rim, testing the temperature before taking a sip.

"Feel like going for a drive?"

"Where?"

"The Presidio."

Fifteen minutes later, Adam was sitting in Randall's van. The sky was grey to the west. They drove north on Divisadero, turning left on California and then right onto Presidio Avenue. Soon they were surrounded by park.

"Until about eleven or twelve years ago, this was an army base." The van rolled past redwood trees and buildings that used to belong to the military. The terrain was beautiful but confusing. They passed a graveyard. "That's the San Francisco National Cemetery. My grandfather's in there. It's one of only two remaining burial places left in San Francisco, if you don't count the tomb of Thomas Starr King, which is just a single grave—or the Columbarium, which isn't your standard burial ground. In the early twentieth century, the city got rid of all the cemeteries."

"They just moved the graves?" Adam sounded bothered by this.

"Yeah. They moved everybody down to Colma," Randall said. "The ghosts of the people who are angry about it cause traffic jams on 280 as you pass by their final resting place during rush hour."

They stopped and parked in a small lot on a bluff. A few people were walking the nearby trails but the place was quiet except for the wind and the surf. There was a concrete structure with some steps leading up to it. They climbed up to what looked like a kind of bunker with large, round features molded in the top.

"Those round parts held mounts for big guns. A whole bunch of these artillery batteries were built around 1900 or so along this part of the coastline. They were meant to defend the city from an enemy attack. Underwater minefields had been planted out there, and the guns were supposed to stop minesweepers from sabotaging the mines."

The wind was cold.

"You think the guys manning those guns out here huddled together for warmth?" Adam asked.

"Undoubtedly."

Randall put his arm around Adam's shoulders. They stood and watched the ships enter the Golden Gate. In the middle distance, the bridge was huge and breathtakingly high above the water.

"Man, I'm really in San Francisco."

"Pretty neat, huh?" said Randall. "I thought you might enjoy this."

"Ever make out on a gun battery before?"

"We could try it. I'm sure it's standard operating procedure."

On the way back to the van, Randall said, "Are you hungry? I was thinking we'd go to Louis'." He pronounced it Louie's. "It's near the Cliff House but cheaper and higher up on the cliff."

"What's the Cliff House?"

"You haven't heard of the Cliff House? It's a famous restaurant near Seal Rocks. It's been around since the 1860s, though it's burned down a couple of times. It's a popular destination and they do a nice brunch. But locals," said Randall with smug chauvinism, "go to Louis'."

When they got to the van, Randall reached in his pocket and froze.

"Shit, I don't believe this. I locked my keys in the van."

"Whoops," said Adam, not unkindly.

"It's okay," said Randall, sounding like it was not okay. "We'll just call Triple A. I'm really sorry about this. I hope it won't be too long. This is really embarrassing. I feel like an idiot."

"Hey, the rear door's unlocked," said Adam.

"Very good. We'll be on our way, then."

Ted had spent almost all Saturday morning on his work laptop at the kitchen table. It had been cool and foggy earlier, but now the sun was out. The problems of CUE weren't going to be untangled in the next hour. He would go do something else—maybe a visit to Lacey's Books would shake out the blahs. Gustavo might be working and Ted could say hello.

After that, he could get something to eat and read a new book.

At Lacey's, Gustavo was at the register when Orion dropped in to invite him to an opening that evening. Orion was a self-actualized, mature artist living life to its fullest potential: creative, athletic, virile, only getting better with time. He considered it his special responsibility to seek out and nurture others like himself. Gustavo was such a lad.

"Good morning, Gustavo!"

"Hey Orion. How's it going?"

"Really well. There's an opening tonight for my friend Seth Borkowski at 20th Street Art Space, and I wondered if you want to come with me."

"Yeah—I'm off at six and should be able to go," said Gustavo. "Let me check in with Jason. He might want to go too."

As Gustavo and Orion were talking, along came Ted Schacter. Ted waved but Gustavo was busy with someone, an attractive stranger he obviously knew. The stranger seemed to be flirting. Ted couldn't very well stare, though there was nothing unnatural in glancing over that way. Just not too often. In a little while, the attractive, self-assured stranger about his own age would leave, and Ted could talk to Gustavo himself. But he was there for the books. He picked one up and leafed through the pages. The stranger was good-looking and fit. Maybe he and Gustavo were good friends. But it was none of Ted's business. He was there to shop.

Suddenly, Ted looked up to notice Orion and Gustavo finishing their conversation. Ted started to walk to the counter, then chuckled under his breath. Thinking too much about a student would be silly. He kept browsing.

Later that evening at 20th Street Art Space, a decent crowd had turned up for Seth Borkowski's opening. On the walls were scenes of buff models posed as costumed superheroes and villains, usually at the moment when it looked like evil might triumph. It wasn't clear what outcome Seth might have been rooting for.

Duane Doyle floated among the pictures and visitors without focusing much on the former or the latter, a vague, mildly inane expression of pleasure on his face, sipping free sparkling wine from a clear plastic cup. At length, he stopped in front of a print and stood gazing at it for a long time.

"Sorry, I don't mean to bother you, but could I ask what you think of it?" The guy talking to Duane had beautiful skin and a worked-out body shown off by a snug, crewneck pullover. When he spoke, in a sad, angsty voice that somehow made him even sexier, he sounded a little like he had a headache.

"It's amazing. The model, the costume, the props, the way it's lit and photographed, the paper. I love weird, intricate, theatrical photos."

"I'm glad someone likes it. Maybe I'll sell something tonight."

"Oh gosh, you're the artist!" Duane laughed. "I'm sorry, I didn't mean to say your photos are weird."

"No need to apologize. They're definitely weird. I'm Seth. I'm so glad you came tonight."

"I'm Duane. Nice to meet you. This is an incredible show."

"Thank you. I can't believe I got it. This place is way too yuppie and hetero for stuff like mine. How did you find out about it?"

"There were some postcards at the camera shop where I work. It looked really interesting."

At the door, Orion was schmoozing a woman with shiny black and burgundy hair and a man in glasses and a gold brocade jacket, telling them all about how he was able to play a small but important role in the development of Seth's career. Orion's buff young companion, Lucas, scanned a remote vista, expertly chewing gum. Gustavo and Jason had seen what looked like wine and wandered off to find some.

"The photos are a trip, huh?" said Gustavo, looking around.

"Yeah," agreed Jason. "I dunno if I like them much."

"Yeah, not really my thing either. They're well done and the dudes are pretty, but it's all a little too shiny."

"They also seem kind of mean," said Jason.

"There's definitely some cruelty going on there, huh?" After a moment, Gustavo added, "And I can't tell whether Seth is S or M."

When Seth found out Duane worked for Hengist Photography, he was delighted. They talked shop and people in common. It turned out they were both fans of a guy who projected retro softcore montages in bars and clubs South of Market and the Castro. Duane had lots of technical questions about Seth's work and how long it took to put together the show, but the gallery was getting more crowded.

Duane said, "I shouldn't keep you too long on such an important evening."

"Listen, I'm really glad you came by," said Seth, still tortured but a little less pained. "Would you like to have a drink sometime?"

On the other side of the room, Jason looked at the people and tried to drink the wine, which wasn't getting any better or colder in the plastic cup. This was his first art opening, another kind of grown-up ritual to figure out. Everyone seemed to know each other. Probably a bunch were friends of the artist. Jason watched as two hot guys in their early thirties talked in front of a piece and pointed to things in it. They were probably saying stuff way over his head. Jason looked at the picture. It was like the photographer looked down on the victim and lusted after the bully.

"The wine's making my mouth kinda sticky," said Gustavo. "You wanna go get some water?"

"Yeah, okay."

As they got in the queue for the bar, one of the humpy early thirties guys Jason had been watching came up and waited in line behind them. At close range, he was even cuter. He saw Jason noticing him and gave him a sexy smile. Gustavo was next at the table. He got two small bottles of water and handed Jason one.

As they walked away, Gustavo said in a low voice, "That dude's pretty, huh? I think he dug us."

Jason smiled the bashful little smile Gustavo liked so much.

Suddenly, Orion appeared with Lucas. Jason tensed up. "Hey, you guys! Let me introduce you to Seth." Orion brought them over to the sexy stranger who had flirted with them a moment ago. He was standing just a few feet away. "Seth, this my friend, Gustavo, and his boyfriend, Jason. I first met Seth in a media course I taught for a semester as a visiting artist in Chicago."

That handsome guy with the nice chest was the artist who made all those cruel images. Maybe they were kind of cool after all. At least the models were handsome.

"You boys are so sweet together," Seth said to Jason and Gustavo. "Maybe you'd let me photograph you sometime."

Jason blushed and smiled.

"Seth, I think you and Gustavo might have a lot in common," said Orion. "I'm glad the two of you could meet."

Lucas kept right on chewing gum.

4

THE MORNING GREY was quickly disappearing, being replaced by a bright, clear sky. Downtown, the streets were already filled with people in every imaginable variation of rainbow-themed outfit, including some that weren't exactly clothes. In an hour, the weather was going to be just warm enough to show off a little.

"Hey, can you do my back?" Adam stood shirtless in the bathroom, trying to coat his upper body evenly in sunscreen before strutting his stuff in the summer light.

"Yeah, sure." Eugene came from the bedroom across the hall and spread some lotion on Adam's shoulder blades. "Sorry if my fingers are cold." When he was done, he took off his shirt and Adam basted him in kind.

"Where are we supposed to meet Randall?" Eugene asked as Adam massaged in the sunscreen.

"He said there's some spot over by 6th Street that he likes. I dunno. We'll find him. He's as tall as a tree. I'll be amazed if I'm able to see anything."

"You wanna walk down there?"

"Yeah, maybe we'd better. The 5 Fulton normally goes straight to Civic Center but the buses are probably all screwed up. Walking seems like more fun anyway."

Duane didn't really have a plan for the day. At work that week, Randall had asked if he would like to come along with him and some friends. Duane said he would let him know, then forgot to decide until the next morning. Instead, he dialed Seth's number on impulse. When Seth answered, he sounded like he had been sleeping. Duane asked if he was going to see the parade.

"I wasn't planning on going," Seth said wearily. "It's just too many people. I can't deal. Too many straight people and gawkers and people from the suburbs. It's like a human zoo and a really ugly one. And people bring their dogs. That has to be so stressful for a dog. Are you going?"

Duane said that was.

"I'm sorry, I shouldn't put it down. I really just can't handle it today. I should probably turn in my gay card or something."

Duane said it was okay, that he'd catch Seth another time.

"I'm really sorry," said Seth.

After they hung up, Duane dialed Randall's number.

"No, it's not too late at all," said Randall. "I'm sure my friends would be pleased to meet you. We'll be on the southeast corner of Market and 6th."

Near Civic Center station on the south side of the street, Gustavo and Jason exchanged hugs with their friends Mike, Troy, and James. The crowds were thick but the boys managed to get partial views through the heads. People walking alongside the floats sometimes threw Mardi Gras beads or candy from plastic buckets. Troy scored a condom. They saw motorcycles, marching bands, activists, corporate sponsors, nightclubs with booming speakers, politicians in vintage convertibles, religious groups, public safety officers, go-go dancers, various allies and alliances. Beautiful bodies more decorative than sensual. Makeup worn like a mask. Feathers, sequins, leather, fun fur. And a whole lot of khaki shorts and t-shirts. Photographers with huge lenses shinnied up lampposts. The low concrete wall around the stairs to the underground offered a better view but also a sheer drop on the other side. On the sidewalk, Gustavo hugged Jason from behind, making their footprint smaller but also keeping them from getting separated in the drifting ranks of spectators.

One long block to the east, Duane made his way through the noise and confusion until he spotted his work buddy, Randall, who was standing with two guys in their early twenties.

"Hey Duane," said Randall. "These are my friends Adam and Eugene. I can't remember if I've said this already but they're visiting for the summer from Brooklyn, New York."

Everybody shook hands, and agreed that the weather was nice and not too cold, though Eugene said how much cooler and less muggy the weather was in San Francisco on that same day of the year. Adam agreed. They asked Duane if he was from San Francisco, and he explained that he had moved from Maryland six years before. Everyone was very polite. They watched the parade quietly for a while.

Then the air started to vibrate with techno as a flatbed with a bunch of muscle boys wearing matching underwear got nearer and nearer: a big name porn studio. It came to a standstill when the parade paused for a moment. The spectators had nothing else to look at, so everyone just stared at the porn models, who weren't all that erotic. After a little a while, Duane laughed. "Gosh, they look bored."

Eugene laughed too. "They're *totally* bored."

"Yeah, they hate this," Adam agreed.

"I can't understand why," said Randall. "Wouldn't you want to listen to a mind-numbing disco thump while standing on a slow-moving truck in the middle of Market Street?"

A few of the models pretended to dance. Most didn't bother.

"Maybe we could throw them something to read," Eugene said.

"Yeah, like a newspaper," said Adam.

Randall suggested that they could call their parade contingent "Pornographers for Journalism."

"Now *that*," said Duane, "would be an amazing float."

At Civic Center Plaza, the Beaux Arts dome of city hall rose grandly amid avenues of booths in all directions. Steve labored under a black canopy emblazoned with the logo of his video company, moving cardboard boxes of DVDs and t-shirts, trying to eat the kielbasa Hector had brought him before it went completely cold. Along with Hector and another of their business partners were two models in neoprene harnesses and butch scanties who were there to help attract visitors. At the moment, it amounted to not much more than a bunch of lookie-loos but that was okay. Just get the name out there. And people watch.

Young people holding hands, tipsy tourists showing a lot of skin, old couples, drag queens, preppies, punks, frumps, kooks, lesbian families, street folks, aunties, hippies, gaggles of silly teens. In a few hours, he and Hector would pack up, head home, feed the cat, make a sandwich, set up the bedroom, take an in-call, eat some ice cream, and go to bed. Lately, Steve had been avoiding the ice cream but today was going to be a long one.

Oliver, his delicate redhead skin shaded by a straw gardener's hat, surveyed the celebration with an expression of blank bewilderment. He wandered through the enormous enterprise, past corporate sponsors, support organizations, souvenirs and crafts, and lines for mystery food and chemical toilets, finally arriving at an enclosure at the eastern end of UN Plaza. Inside, a small band played psychedelic rock, and people sat on the grass in costume, talking and chilling out.

He walked around for a while, then sat down and watched everything around him. This was where the cool stuff was happening, but it was still confusing. Some of the glitter-jeweled faces were completely disguised. Tutus and crinolines on all genders. Half-naked hippie boys. A young man in a strangely crisp gingham shirt so movie star handsome it was hard not to stare. Lots of people obviously knew each other. No one spoke to Oliver, but at no point did he approach someone to talk to. He never even noticed all the guys who paused to admire his copper-gold curls and innocent, pale grey eyes. After a while, he got up to go, just missing Randall.

"This is always the best part," said Duane. He and Randall and the two New Yorkers had found their way to the little semi-private world of all the fun freaks. Adam and Eugene had already shed their shirts, pulling them through a belt loop. This was what they came for. Duane waved to a lavender and blue fairy queen he knew who gave him a hug. In the small stage area, some sexy guitar boy was grooving on a long, trippy solo. The guys found a spot on the lawn near a tree.

Eugene looked over and noticed a cute shirtless guy with a lean body and spiky, medium-brown hair sitting with some friends. He was older than Eugene by about three or four years. He kept glancing over and breaking into an irresistible grin.

Adam sat half-naked, cross-legged on his bit of grass in the middle of the fairground in the middle of the city. In the shade, the air was only just warm enough to be comfortable on bare skin. The weather took some getting used to, but it sparkled. Randall was telling a story about some guy he knew who had a funny penis. Nearby, a boy with a beautiful smile was giving Eugene the eye. Duane started dancing by himself. He was goofy but definitely hot. Adam got up and danced with him. In a little while, Adam and Duane boogied over to Randall and pulled him to his feet.

"Having fun?" said the guy with spiky hair to Eugene.

"Yeah, you know, I think I am," Eugene replied, as if he had just at that moment checked in with himself and realized that the whole scene was agreeing with him very nicely. "I'm visiting from New York. This is pretty amazing."

"Welcome, visitor from New York. Are you staying long?"

"My buddy and I are here for the summer. We just graduated from college and wanted a little time for some fun."

"Sounds great. Is the friend a boyfriend?"

"Nah, just a friend."

The guy with the spiky hair's name was Cody.

"Nice to meet you, Cody. I'm Eugene."

"Even your name is sexy," said Cody.

"Man," laughed Eugene, "you gotta be kidding me. You're the one with the sexy name."

"No, really—on you, it's, I dunno... manly." Cody raised an eyebrow and deepened his voice: "Eu-*gene*."

"Ha! That's awesome."

Gustavo and Jason and Mike and Troy and James sat on the shaded lawn inside the magic enclosure checking out the other boys. Mike asked how they could snag some of those cuties wearing nothing but undies, tutus, and boots. James didn't know but he sure wanted one. There was a professionally handsome guy in a gingham shirt. Gustavo pointed out a tall fellow he recognized from school who was dancing with some other guys. A fawn-like dude with Kelly green hair walked by.

"The boy with green hair!" said Troy.

"I love that movie," Gustavo said with a grin.

Nobody else had seen it.

"Okay," said Gustavo, "it goes like this. There's this kid whose parents are killed doing rescue aid in World War II. He's rejected by one crappy relative after another until finally he's taken in by an old Irish actor who works as a singing waiter. One day, the kid looks in the mirror and his hair's turned bright green. At first, it's funny, but pretty soon, he realizes he has a problem. Nobody's ever seen green hair. People who liked and accepted him before start freaking out and treating him like a pariah."

The guys were quiet for a while.

Then Mike said, "Well I guess it must've turned out okay since that's him over there."

Randall sat down on the grass again and yawned. "Are you gentlemen hungry?"

"Extremely," said Adam.

"Yeah, me too," said Duane. "I was thinking Indian food."

Eugene and Cody were talking quietly. The friends Cody arrived with were giving him some space. Adam leaned toward Eugene with a grin. "Hey, Randall, Duane and I are going for Indian food. You boys coming?"

"I think," said Eugene, "we're gonna make our own plans."

Cody had suggested a taqueria not far from Eugene and Adam's pad, so they walked leisurely in that direction.

"Any plans for after San Francisco?"

"I've been working as a personal trainer, which is great, but I think I'm going to apply to a physical therapy program."

"Sounds like a fine occupation."

"What do you do?"

"I'm a baritone."

"You mean like a singer?"

"Yup. Opera singer."

"Whoa—that's really amazing. I've never met an opera singer." Cody didn't seem anything like Pavarotti.

"I do musical theater, too. But classical music was what I went to school for. And there are other songs I only sing in the shower."

"So how did you get into singing?"

"The arts are a big deal in my family. Everybody does something. Some of us do two or three things."

"Interesting," said Eugene. "I play guitar, but I'm not all that serious."

"But that's making music. What kind of stuff do you play?"

"Mostly rock and folk rock. I'm starting to get interested in Hawaiian slack-key guitar since I met a guy who knows a lot about it."

"And you want to become a physical therapist?"

"Yeah, fitness training is fine for now, but I think rehabilitation is really what interests me."

"You have an amazing body."

"Thanks—you look great too."

"Must be all the tacos I eat," said Cody. "The food at the place we're going to is really good."

Somewhere in the hillside maze of Eureka Valley streets west of the Castro, three couples who called themselves the League of Lavender Engineers convened for a special dinner. Chuck, the lone lawyer in the group, coined the name. He was a patent attorney who worked with tech clients, and the others agreed that he was not merely an honorary member but an essential one. Chuck was putting the finishing touches on a platter of hors d'oeuvres while Richard poured Pinot noir. ("Sonoma

Coast?" "Willamette Valley.") The hosts had worked most of the afternoon on the preparations, but then they hadn't gone to the parade in years anyway. Kyle and Mark and Aaron and Jeff hadn't gone that day either. But this was still a holiday.

Kyle's new game release was doing pretty well. He was the youngest, if only by a few years. Richard and Chuck were the oldest, and they joked about being a couple of squares. The good life meant being in a secure position to pursue one's interests in peace. They talked of getting a dog, though Richard wondered if it would be happy if they were gone all day then went to the symphony. Or on a long trip. They liked to travel. Jeff and Aaron were planning a trip to the desert with the telescope. Richard and Chuck said they'd like to join them sometime. Some of Richard's best photos were of Death Valley.

Aaron and Jeff had almost finished renovating the first floor of their Noe Valley shoebox Victorian. They installed the wine cellar next to Jeff's office, naturally. Mark recently started collecting bourbon and was thinking about getting some sort of cabinet, but he was afraid he might outgrow it immediately. Richard asked if Mark knew about the new, high-end liquor store downtown, and Mark did.

Mark and Kyle had gone to a baseball game that week. Did anyone think the boys would turn the season around? Polite interest from the group, suspended when Chuck put down a tray of something good to eat.

What was everyone doing for the Fourth? Aaron and Jeff wanted to show off their garden, and Richard said he'd be happy to see it. They could walk over. Besides, even on their hill, it was too foggy and too far away to see any fireworks.

But the view from the room was magical. Richard couldn't resist a quick photo for the millionth time. Even with that very tall building they were constructing in the wrong place, the city looked gorgeous in the summer evening light. Now that the solstice had passed, the days would be getting shorter. Maybe not perceptibly at first. Soon it would be fall. Someone's niece was going to the blue and gold school; someone's nephew to the red and white one. That freshman class was the future of the species. Chuck told everyone to pick up his glass and head to the table.

Adam was full of Indian food, slouching in a squarish armchair in the living room which was his bedroom at night. Randall, also stuffed, flopped on the sofa, which had not yet been turned into a bed. They were recapping the day and trying to make themselves take a shower to wash off the sunscreen. Their arms and legs had turned to sandbags.

"I have glitter stuck to the weirdest places," Randall said with a groan.

"And you didn't even take your shirt off."

"Yeah, I know."

"We should shower."

"Yes, we should."

Neither of them moved.

"Duane's hot," said Adam. "It was fun dancing with him. You guys ever mess around?"

Randall shook his head. "He's my work buddy. It would be incest."

Adam nodded.

They talked about all the other dudes they saw that day and how beautiful they all were. Some of the flirtations were agony. It was a pity they couldn't get freaky right there in the middle of the event.

Then Adam said, "Have you ever been in a three-way?"

"A couple of times. You?"

"No. I'd like to try one."

"I'd be up for that," said Randall.

"Do you know someone who'd be into it?"

"Maybe so. I could invite my friend Oliver over later this week."

"What's he like?"

"I think you'd like him. He's a very nice guy, though he can be a little quiet."

In Eugene's room, Cody handed over a pipe full of marijuana and a lighter. They were chilling naked on the floor. Eugene took a hit and just managed to avoid burning his lungs. "This is really good. I'm such a lightweight, though. It's got me wasted."

"I'm sorry."

"No, no—I'm having fun. I just don't do this very often."

"Mr. Fitness Trainer."

Eugene chuckled. "Hey, I know plenty of stoners at the gym. But yeah, you could say I've got a wholesome, healthy lifestyle going on."

"Did you bring your guitar from New York?"

"No. Now I'm wishing I had, but we just wanted to throw a couple of things in a bag and take off."

"What would you play if you had a guitar right now?"

"I dunno—I'm probably too high to play anything. But on weed like this, it would probably turn out soft and introspective."

"That was my music as a teenager," said Cody. "My friends and I would sit around listening to psychedelic rock albums and get all quiet."

"I can totally see you as a moody rocker boy," Eugene said with a laugh. "Very different from an opera singer."

"I didn't know I was an opera singer yet, though I was already paying attention to that kind of music."

"Would you sing something for me?"

"I'm most definitely too high for that right now. But if you like Benjamin Britten, I'll be singing something in a concert coming up at the conservatory. It's part of a program I'm in for young artists trying to build a career. Maybe you'd like to come. But it'll be this big classical thing, and I won't be the only act on the bill. I won't be offended if you say no."

"I'd love to hear you sing," said Eugene.

5

MONDAY MORNING. Randall had been slightly behind schedule and made himself later still by buying a latte. To add insult to self-inflicted injury, the coffee was cold by the time he slunk into Literature of the Counterculture at 10:17, trying to look as small as possible. Professor Ellen Russo noticed this and remarked that if he was late again, he could bring a coffee for her too—decaf double cap. If he had turned around, he would've seen classmate Gustavo Cortez trying to suppress a grin.

The seminar topic of the week was the Beat Generation in San Francisco. Ellen wrote the name *Sal Mariano* on the board. "Let's start with an early poem. Last time, I gave you—" Ellen flipped over a page of notes—'Visions of Greenbaum.' Does somebody feel like reading?"

Randall volunteered since he was late to class.

> *I float through my window at twilight*
> *digging the Peter & Paul bong*
> *of the bells, and know it's jazz-*
> *time and in that hazy the Square*

goes all crazy clear for me
like an eye for calzone pie-
dough pillow moon-
saxophone is singing, swingle-ing
Nirvana-clouds, brains
jazzing jagged, second sight
is mine tonight & I will speak bongos
in tongues of skoo ba dee boo
galaxy in blue twilight, beat-
ing open doorways Grant Ave gin mill
filled with my own blatting blowing flowing
all sound—I'll be cool
cat & cool green catnip
& Yerba Buena
I'll be there before begot
the twilight phantoms
Let me go on
scatting, skating
my beat bongos sound ages
& recorded in stone like
the rings of redwoods & crazy seabeds

When he had finished, Ellen said, "Nice, Randall. Anybody wanna say anything about it?"

"Sal is one crazy cat," said Randall.

Ellen chuckled. "Yeah, a little too crazy with the Beat lingo, maybe. But it's an early one. What else?"

Another student raised her hand. "It's set in North Beach."

"That's right," said Ellen. "In his twenties, he worked in his family's grape business in Napa, and drove to San Francisco to go to jazz shows. As he spent more time in the city, he found other Beat writers who influenced his first poems."

Gustavo raised his hand. "I believe the title refers to Alvin Greenbaum."

"Correct. The poem is inspired by a friendship between the two poets, and was written when Mariano first moved in with Greenbaum on Telegraph Hill. Some Greenbaum biographers have said that the two had a brief sexual relationship as well, though in those days," Ellen said with a smile, "I doubt anyone in that bunch was keeping score."

As class ended and Randall was packing up to go, Gustavo went over to talk to him.

"I liked the way you read that poem."

"Thanks," said Randall. "You're too kind. I think I dig Sal Mariano."

"At the moment, he's my favorite Beat. I'm super excited to be taking this seminar."

"So am I. I had to rearrange my work schedule so I could be here—not that I'd seem very grateful for it today, as I couldn't manage to arrive on time."

Gustavo laughed. "Hey, I'm only barely on time because I can walk here. If I had to take Muni, forget it. Listen, I hope this isn't too personal, but do you write anything at all?"

"Sometimes," Randall admitted guardedly. "Why do you ask?"

"The bookstore where I work is having an open mic next week, and I'm wondering if you'd like to come." Gustavo handed him a flyer from his messenger bag. "It would be great if you'd read something, but no pressure. We'd be happy if you just came to listen."

"Thanks, I'm really flattered to be asked to read. I don't know if I'll have anything ready, but I'll definitely think about it."

"Great. And maybe you'll come anyway whether you read something or not."

"It's not a poetry slam, is it?"

"Haha—no, it's not a poetry slam. And no poets will be slammed. Unless they want to be."

"All right. I'll keep that in mind in case I'm in the mood," said Randall with a crooked smile.

"Hey, you never know when you're gonna need a good slam, right?"

"You said it, brother."

"How's it going, Adam?" Ted asked.

"Okay. I ought to be through with this drawer of ancient history by noon." Adam frowned. "So tell me again who wants you to do this departmental review? I get why you might be asked to do one, but I forget what you said about it."

"The individual academic departments report to the vice president of academic affairs—she's our chief academic officer," Ted explained. "The review allows the college to understand how the program does what it does, its instructional needs, and how that translates to our budget. But it also gets reported to an accrediting agency which is accountable to the federal government."

What Ted didn't say to Adam was that the College for the Urban Environment was also compiling data because the institution was trying to understand whether it could correct course. CUE and its campus had played a recognizable part in the history of the city in the '70s, but the school never had a substantial endowment. Real estate costs in the city were rising, enrollments were declining, and CUE's recent mismanagement now threatened its survival.

Ted and his colleagues were hoping that the solution would come in the form of a merger with a small, private institution called Yerba Buena University. The two schools were in talks, but it wasn't a done deal.

"I can see why you say being director of the program is a hassle," said Adam.

"Yeah, in addition to the long hours, there's some really dull crap."

"Why did you agree to do it?"

"Well, sometimes," Ted said with a sad smile, "you're the most logical person for the job."

"When did you decide to become a teacher?"

"For an egghead like me, it's one of the standard options. You enter grad school and hopefully you come out the other side with one of the better academic jobs, though there are plenty of mediocre ones. I guess I could have tried to become a full-time writer or a journalist if I'd been luckier, more determined or less risk averse. But somehow, I always imagined I'd be a teacher of some kind. At one point, I thought I might teach high school but ended up in higher ed instead, probably because for some reason, I seem to be good at reading and writing things no one else wants to read. Why do you ask? You aren't thinking of going to grad school, are you?"

"Is it really that bad?"

"Heheh—no, it's not. I just asked because you don't seem like you'd want to."

"And I don't, or at least I don't think so. I'm just trying to figure out some things, like when and how my actual life begins."

"You'll know soon enough. Maybe sooner. But right now is your life too. Try to enjoy the summer."

Adam applied Ted's advice as directly as he knew how by going to Randall's that evening for some no-strings fun. They had decided Randall would invite his friend Oliver so the three boys might get to know each other in an intimate way. After a bite to eat and a shower, Adam went to Duboce Park to get the N Judah. When the streetcar arrived, it was full of people but enough of them exited to make a little room. He climbed in.

They went through a tunnel, and on the other side, Adam was in a different San Francisco. He passed a steep hill with a hospital on it to the south, then a busy retail area several blocks long. It all looked very friendly and a bit reminiscent of some of the mellower neighborhoods back home. As he got closer to the beach, he saw mostly low stucco houses. The signs were hard to make out through the windows of the moving streetcar, but he managed to pull the cord within a couple of blocks of Randall's place. He found the address without too much trouble and rang a doorbell next to the side door near the garage. In a moment, Randall appeared, looking distracted.

"Greetings. Please come in."

A bicycle with a helmet hanging on it was leaning against the wall outside the apartment door. Randall led Adam inside. The place had been straightened up and hardly looked crazy at all. Even the desk looked a little better. Sitting in a chair was a handsome guy about Adam's age with a frizzy, curly, red-gold ponytail and serious grey eyes with nearly invisible lashes. When he stood, he was about five foot nine—taller than Adam but lighter in build.

"Adam, this is Oliver. Oliver, this is Adam."

Oliver was reserved but smiled when they shook hands. "Nice to meet you."

"Adam is visiting from Brooklyn, New York for the summer," Randall added.

"I've heard a lot about Brooklyn," said Oliver, warming a little. "It seems like an interesting place."

"Yeah, though I'm not necessarily from the most interesting part of it. Except for *Saturday Night Fever.*" That got a laugh.

Adam mentioned he had a temp job at College of the Urban Environment, and Oliver said he worked at Grateful Peas Grocery in the Mission.

"I don't know the city very well yet," said Adam, "but that sounds like an organic foods store."

"Yeah, it is."

Randall talked a little about how he and Oliver met through Green Rainbow, which he described as a fairly typical environmental group that organized talks, demonstrations, and social events only everyone was some sort of non-hetero. That got a laugh too.

While everyone was still smiling, Adam said, "So, you fellas wanna get naked?"

Oliver froze.

"I think I just made a mistake," said Adam.

"I gotta go." Oliver headed for the door.

"Oliver, please don't leave," said Randall. "I'm afraid I've caused a terrible misunderstanding."

But Oliver grabbed his bike and was gone.

After Oliver had shown himself out, Randall trudged to the kitchen and brought back a bottle and couple of glasses.

"I am a banana-head." He poured himself a finger of booze.

"You made a mistake," said Adam, pouring some for himself.

"Somehow I thought he'd go for it."

"Well, maybe not everyone's a dog like we are."

"I should've told him in the first place why we wanted him to come over."

"Yeah, that would've been better. But you spoke up and said you were sorry when things went all stupid."

"I'm deeply embarrassed."

"I know how you feel."

"I'm really sorry we upset him."

"So am I."

"I was thinking with my penis. It's not the right organ for that."

"No, it's not. It's a beautiful thing otherwise, though."

"Yes. Yes, it is."

6

THE DAY WAS bright and windy, and the air downtown seemed electric, a perfect time to be out in the city. Seth was already at the museum when Duane arrived. He was in a leather car coat and sunglasses, standing against the wall, beautiful as ever, sort of pouty. But then he saw Duane and smiled.

"Hey. It's good to see you."

"It's good to see you, too," said Duane. "You're looking very... very glamorous."

"Ugh, I really need the shades right now. It's one of those days when the light is unbearable. I think I have photophobia, which is a pretty obnoxious thing for a photographer to have."

Duane laughed. "Sorry, that sounds really terrible."

"Go ahead and laugh. I think it's pretty funny too."

They went inside and stood in line for admission. Seth hadn't been there in several months and wondered if the museum had rotated the permanent collection lately. It seemed like they'd had the same pieces up for a while. Duane watched the mobile spinning high over their heads. The lobby was scented with espresso and buttery pastry from the café. Seth took off his shades.

At the entrance to the special exhibition galleries, the name of a twentieth century pop artist appeared in big letters on the wall. Inside were big, broadly painted canvases in bright colors, mostly of sexy guys. Duane liked one of a hunky jock with a broad nose and jug ears sitting on a sofa with one bare foot on the table in front of him: *Brian*.

"I feel like he's going to stomp on my face," said Seth. "But he's sexy."

Duane was amused and a little horrified. "Um, gee, he just looks cute and cuddly to me."

"Yeah, he'd be cute and cuddly while he beat me up. But thugs are definitely hot."

There was a painting of a naked guy in bed, partly draped by a sheet, sleeping under an open window with the light of the moon coming in. Seth said, "That sort of reminds me of a werewolf scene I've been thinking about doing for a while."

"A photo, you mean?"

"Yeah. I'll get a boy to wear a mask and be the werewolf, and another to be the beautiful victim."

"The beautiful victim doesn't get eaten, does he?" Duane laughed but sounded concerned.

"Not in the photo, anyway. The werewolf would be standing over the boy, who's asleep, or he fell and can't get away. I haven't decided yet."

"That's sorta scary, but I guess it's the kind of photo you go for."

"Yeah, it is," said Seth, a little self-consciously. "Well, maybe the beautiful victim wouldn't get eaten. And the werewolf could be carrying condoms."

They wandered on to the permanent collections, strolling past action painting frenzies and color field space-outs.

"Would you let me photograph you?" asked Seth. "I don't how you'd feel about doing that, but I think you'd make a good model."

"Gee, I dunno. Would I be a victim of the werewolf?"

"No," Seth said with a laugh. "I wouldn't ask you to be the victim of the werewolf. I wasn't thinking about a costumed project or anything like that. I'd just like to photograph you as you."

Duane said he was flattered and might enjoy modeling. Seth was sort of messed up and said terrible, nasty things, but he was smart and had an amazing eye. He was also really easy on the eyes.

On the way to the photo galleries, Seth said, "Would you want to be the werewolf instead?"

"Ha! I'm trying really hard to imagine myself ripping someone's heart out. I guess if I were wearing the mask so I wouldn't have to look all scary, that might be okay. I'm not really an in-front-of-the-camera person, though I don't mind being photographed."

"So you're okay with being photographed as yourself?"

"Yeah," said Duane. "Maybe posing for someone could be interesting."

"Not a star," said Seth. "That's sexy. The models I work with are really stuck up. Not all, but enough of them. But they're definitely pretty. And the camera sure loves the stuck-up boys. Something happens when they get in front of a lens. It's like they've found their secret lover."

A bunch of young tourists came in giggling.

Duane said, "Sometimes I've wondered what it would be like to pose for a figure drawing class. That seems like it could be an easy, interesting way to make money."

"The money isn't that good, and it's sort of exploitive, but at least you don't have to do much. When I took figure drawing classes in school, they always used the same weird, exhibitionistic people. It was never anybody you wanted to look at, much less draw. But your job is way better than that. You work with photo equipment, right?"

"Yeah, sales and rentals. Photo processing too. But it's just sort of a job for right now. I feel like I need to go back to school and focus on a career."

"Like what?"

"I dunno—that's my problem. I guess it would be some kind of art school."

"You don't need what they're teaching in those places."

"Why not? I feel like I need more technical knowledge."

"What you're doing right now requires highly technical knowledge."

"Yeah, I guess so. I pick up stuff like that pretty quickly. But I don't really know how to think about a career. I'm such a dork when it comes to that kind of thing. I'm a dork about a lot of things, come to think of it."

"Dorkiness can be hot."

At seven thirty, Adam had just finished eating after a hard leg workout and was about to take a shower when Randall showed up at the door without warning.

"I'd like you to help me with something."

"Arright, but I just came from the gym. I'm probably not smelling too good."

"You smell great. Let me show you something." Randall opened his briefcase, which contained masking tape and a rolled sheet of discarded photo paper, which he unfurled briefly to show the letters and numerals of a makeshift Ouija board drawn with a marker.

"You want me to help you with a séance?!"

"Something like that."

"Okay sure, why not. So who or what are you séance-ing?"

"I am trying to determine the whereabouts of a Beat poet named Sal Mariano."

"Is this person dead?"

Randall raised his eyebrows. "Good question. Nobody seems to be sure, or at least nothing I've read mentions it. If he's alive, he's about seventy-nine years old. There's nothing I've found anywhere that says he died or wrecked his life or anything like that. He might still be out there somewhere."

"He's a famous writer, and he just faded away?"

"Well, semi-famous. I don't know if anyone reads him much anymore, which could explain how he seems to have faded into obscurity. I'm guessing he didn't actually vanish into thin air, but you never know."

"So you're gonna try to summon him?"

"Not exactly. He was friends with this other poet named Roger Dunstan who was a spiritualist, and Dunstan is really dead, or so we have every reason to believe. I figured we'd try to make contact with him instead as sort of a spirit guide. Either that or this astrologer and swinger named Gaveston Arnold who hung out with the Beats. One of those people should be able to tell us what happened to Sal. That is, if our very long-distance phone call goes through, and I don't really believe it will."

"I'm not sure I do either," said Adam, "but how's it supposed to work?"

"We ask the spirit of the departed a question, and the answer gets spelled out on the board. There's supposed to be this little thing that rolls over the board and points at the letters. I figured we'd use an upside-down glass instead. Apparently, you can do that."

They went into the kitchen and found a lowball glass, which they agreed was appropriate for a Beat poet.

"Now what?" said Adam.

"I'm not an expert in contacting the dead, but I think we sit on the floor."

"We could use the coffee table."

They went into the adjacent living room, which was Adam's

bedroom at night, and they cleared the clutter from the glass coffee table top. Randall spread out his big sheet of paper, the edges of which he fastened to the table with long strips of tape. They tried to get near enough to reach the writing on the board comfortably while sitting cross-legged. It was awkward. In addition to the letters and numbers, Randall had written the words "Yes," "No," "Maybe" and "Goodbye."

"It seems kind of plain," said Adam. "Should it have some planetary symbols or something?"

"You're right," said Randall. "Let's see...." He took a felt tip pen from the briefcase and sketched a sun and a crescent moon. It still looked bare, so he added some asterisk stars and a peace symbol for good measure. "There—how's that?"

"Beautiful," said Adam.

"Now we're supposed to put the fingertips of both hands lightly on the glass," instructed Randall. "It's supposed to travel on its own without pushing." They both rested a few fingertips of each hand lightly on the base of the upturned whisky glass.

"Now what?" said Adam.

"We ask a question," said Randall. He cleared his throat. "Spirit of Roger Dunstan, are you among us?"

Nothing happened. Randall was unfazed. He repeated the question and still nothing happened.

"We'll try the other guy. Spirit of Gaveston Arnold, are you among us?"

The glass moved to "Yes."

"No pushing," said Adam.

"I'm not," said Randall. "Or at least I didn't mean to."

"Okay, ask something else."

"Gaveston Arnold, is Sal Mariano still alive?"

The glass moved to "Maybe."

"So we have a definite 'maybe,'" said Randall. "Gaveston Arnold, is Sal Mariano living in San Francisco?"

The glass moved again to "Maybe."

"Gaveston Arnold," said Randall, "should we go have a beer right about now?"

The glass moved to "Yes."

Adam agreed that a beer sounded good but he needed a shower first.

"I can wash your back if you want," said Randall.

As the boys were getting undressed, Adam asked, "What do you think happened to Mariano?"

"I dunno, really. I'd like to think he's alive and right here in San Francisco. But he could be anywhere."

7

MONDAY BEFORE DAWN, dark waves rolled over the sand at Ocean Beach. The bakers arrived at work and switched the coffee on. Raccoon gangs finished up for the night and went home to bed. Sanitation trucks came roaring and snorting through residential streets, devouring metal, glass, and garbage. The songbirds warmed up in a grand chorus. Lamps in bedrooms made gold rectangles in the deep blue haze. Dog walkers performed their daily obligation. Newspapers landed on doorsteps and walkways. BART and Muni rumbled through their tunnels. Dim light appeared in the sky. The old man in the laundromat cleaned the floor. Garage doors opened and cars crept out, rolling blind past the joggers.

Dawn rose over the East Bay Hills. Office workers with backpacks and briefcases left for downtown. Ravens conversed from the housetops as the coyotes found a place to hide. Ships entered the Golden Gate, and old folks practiced tai chi in the parks. Richard of the League of Lavender Engineers bought a cup of tea. Jason got off the bus downtown a little breathless but on time. Roadwork diverted a lane of traffic on Folsom Street. Yellow backhoes tore at the ground while landladies

swept at fallen leaves. Trolley bus poles popped off the over-
head wires at 16th and Potrero. Sirens wailed and alarms
squawked.

Eugene showed Steve the pornographer how to punch a
speed bag. The MFA office sat down to work. Young mothers
pushed their strollers. Crane-loads of steel beams swung
through the air. Duane arrived at Hengist Photography. Day
camp kids took swimming lessons. Gustavo and Randall took
their seats for Literature of the Counterculture with Ellen
Russo. Adam excused himself to run an errand. Traffic bounced
over cracked roads in the Mission. Parking control officers
issued citations. Oliver finished ringing up a customer.

Oliver turned to greet the next person in line and it was
Adam. Adam looked at him for a moment, placed a small sheet
of folded notepaper with writing inside on the check stand and
walked away. Oliver picked up the folded paper and looked out
the front of the store. Then he had to help another customer, so
he put the paper in the pocket of his apron.

Downtown in his silicon tower, Richard Corwin ate the turkey
sandwich and apple he had brought from home. When he was
done, he had enough time to run out for a moment to buy a
camera battery and maybe browse some lenses at his favorite
store.

Hengist, a wide, three-story building, was already bustling
with people coming and going. The shelves were filled with all
the exciting things a professional or amateur photographer
might need or want. Duane and Melissa were busy showing
equipment from the glass cases and grabbing stock from
drawers behind the counter. Richard came in and looked
briefly at tripods, moving on to a display of gimbals before
going over to the lenses. Duane went over to him and was very
friendly, remembering him from a previous visit. While Duane

fetched the battery, Richard browsed the items in the case. This was why there was a downtown. This was why he lived in the City. When Duane came back, he asked if Richard would like a closer look at any of the lenses. Richard said he had to get back to work but he could take a minute or two. Duane was happy to talk about them and compare. There was no rush, no sales pressure. Richard said he'd be back after he had thought it over.

Later in the day, Randall asked Adam to meet him for a drink near CUE after work. It was in the wrong direction for Randall, but he had said it was important. Adam showed up first and ordered a beer. He'd already had some stress earlier when he dropped off a note for Oliver that said he was sorry, without putting the blame on Randall for being a banana-head, and that Adam was embarrassed for himself about the incident and that he wished Oliver the best.

Randall came in a couple minutes after looking serious. After he asked how Adam was doing, he got to the point.

"Hengist Photography is closing at the end of August."

Adam was stunned. "How can they close?"

"Conrad says he's too old and just can't do it anymore."

"There's gotta be someone who'd buy that business."

"Apparently not, at least not for the moment." Randall ordered a beer.

"Man, I'm totally floored."

"Yeah, I know what you mean," said Randall.

"I'm sorry."

"Thanks. I am officially in the market as of right now."

They sat in silence while the bartender poured Randall's pint and set it in front of him. Randall paid and sipped without even looking at the glass.

"Do you know what you're gonna do?"

"I might try to find a spot at another camera shop, though with all of us looking, that might be a little tricky. Duane said he might do something completely different, though. I dunno —I'll probably be okay. I just hate having that kind of thing unsettled. And I really don't need to go job hunting right now."

"Hengist closing is a loss for the whole city."

"Exactly. It really means a lot to me to know you understand that."

"Man, I'm really sorry."

Randall watched the ceiling fan in the mirror behind the bar. After a while, he said, "Look, since we're sitting here, there's something I've been meaning to ask you about."

"Okay."

"Spending time with you these past few weeks has been really exciting. I'd like to find the right person to get serious with, and I'm wondering if you'd like to take it to the next level." He wore a look of cautious optimism.

Adam took a deep breath. "Randall, my friend, you just met me. I don't even know how long I'm gonna be in San Francisco. But more to the point, something tells me we're not boyfriends."

"Damn. I thought we had a pretty good thing going." He was visibly disappointed but managed a smirk all the same.

"Well, it's just not that particular thing. I'm sorry. I feel like a jerk having to say that on a day when you've already had really terrible news."

Randall laughed. "Yeah, well, I did ask."

They talked for a little while longer, agreeing that they'd see each other around, then went their separate ways.

"What a day," said Eugene when Adam told him what had happened. "So he wanted to get serious after knowing you for only... how long have we been here now, a few weeks?"

"Yeah. And that pretty much tells you everything you need to know. He's a smart guy, but he heads off in his own weird direction." Adam sighed. "Anyway, enough about that. Is tonight Cody's concert?"

"Yeah. I'd better get dressed and get out of here."

"Where is it again?"

"At the conservatory."

"That sounds like a pretty big deal."

"Yeah, I wasn't expecting to meet an up-and-coming classical musician. Maybe I should get some dressier clothes for this trip if I'm going to be going to concerts like this."

"Yeah, really. And you don't even go out at night all that much."

"I know. Hopefully I won't be too long past my bedtime."

"Have fun, man. You found a good one."

Gustavo was stacking books on a sale table when Ted walked into Lacey's.

"Hey Ted!"

"Hey Gustavo!"

"You gonna come to our open mic a little later?"

"I'd really love to, but I can't. Some friends are having me over for dinner." Ted let it show that he was disappointed or at least didn't want to turn Gustavo down. But he was spending a little too much time at that bookstore anyway. "Will you be reading any of your stuff?"

"Yeah, if there's time. Since I work here, I don't wanna hog the floor. If I don't get a turn, no big deal. There'll be other open mics."

"Well, that's good. I'd hate to miss out forever."

The staff had already elected Gustavo to be the emcee, so he had a lot to do even if he didn't read. And he had to help get the store ready. Lacey's would close for an hour to give everyone a break. Tables in the middle of the room needed to be moved to open up the floor. There were chairs and a sound system to set up. The last event was a big success, so they were expecting a crowd.

At a bar up the street, Randall was looking at the piece he had practiced at home over the last few days, carefully chosen from a three-ring notebook of his better efforts. The Beat-inspired story he had selected for a monologue was about five minutes long when he rehearsed it a few times. Now he was having a beer and one last look at the text in its folder before heading over to Lacey's. He hadn't been to an open mic before, let alone performed at one.

On the sidewalk outside Lacey's, people were gathering, finishing up coffees, and hanging on to conversations just a while longer. Jason, having come from work in his button-down shirt, laptop slung around his neck, watched the crowd before going in to find a seat. Along came a group of sexy punk boys— cool, arty types that almost could've been from another planet. They made Jason sigh. He was about to follow them in when Orion showed up with three other guys at the entrance. There was always a crew. Jason hung back a bit and waited for them to pass.

Randall arrived and took a chair near the door, a little off to one side. Gustavo was standing at the front, talking to someone. He noticed Randall and waved. The audience chatter turned into applause and whistles when Gustavo stepped up to the microphone.

"Hey everybody—thanks for coming out on a school night. Welcome to Open Mic at Lacey's. We really appreciate seeing you here. First up tonight is our good friend, Valerie Jamison. Everybody give a warm welcome to Val."

Val turned out to be a tall young woman with a guitar. She sang a witty three-song folk set that got a huge hand. Next was a hippie-ish woman with lots of long, wispy, white hair and fiery poetry. A red-nosed dude in an aloha shirt and a fedora played some guitar blues. A sharply dressed, mid-forties guy read a noir piece set in Hong Kong that blew everyone away. The evening was going well.

At the break, Jason reached into the outer pocket of his laptop bag for some big cookies he bought on the way, then waded through the people to Gustavo.

"Hey you," Gustavo said with a hello kiss. "It's a pretty good show, huh?"

"It's great!" Jason's eyes were shining. This was the San Francisco he had come looking for. "Are you hungry? I brought a couple of cookies from the café."

"Yeah—let's take 'em out front. I wanna get out of here for a minute anyway."

On the sidewalk, Jason held the paper bag open for Gustavo, who pulled out a big oatmeal cookie and started eating.

"Mmm..." he mumbled, munching, "thank you, baby."

Jason yawned and said he was glad for the cool night air because he was tired. He bit into his cookie.

"Don't feel like you have to stay. Go home and get some rest if you need to."

Jason crunched his cookie for a moment, then said, "I can hang out a little longer. You haven't read your poem yet."

"Well, it's up to you," said Gustavo. "But don't feel like you have to stick it out for me if you're falling asleep. There'll be other readings."

"I'm having fun. I want to stay."

Just then, Orion and his boys came out of the bookstore and waved to Gustavo. Jason ate a little faster.

When they returned from the break, the audience was warmed up and ready to get started. It was Randall's turn at the mic.

"Hello everyone. This is a piece I call 'Underwear.'" *Stanley* needed to buy some underwear. *So he mounted himself into his pale blue station wagon, a land boat the size of a studio apartment, and sat down on the cloth and polyvinyl chloride upholstery.* Never smoke in the car. Never leave anything at all in the car. *Underneath his clothes, he was still wearing his old underpants and undershirt, wearing out by the second, threadbare and just perceptibly disintegrating into lint to blow on the wind along with the dust of ancient Rome. By God, you had to wear some kind of underwear. His dog didn't care about Stanley's underwear, but Stanley did. Say whatever else you would, at least it was absolutely sanitary.*

He drove downtown and chose one of the better parking lots. It was a very good parking lot where good people parked good cars. He went into a department store, looking for underwear. Underwear made for men. He walked toward Men's Furnishings and cautiously eyeballed the packages on the shelves, some bearing photos of headless torsos with bellies of granite and pectorals that could crush walnuts. Other packages showed photos of mannequin-like masculine-gendered beings who could have been standing around the water cooler except there was no water cooler and they had no clothes except underwear. Others still had line drawings of nothing but underwear.

A roly-poly salesman with a yellow tie and shiny eyeglasses and a few strands of hair left on top of his shiny head appeared, all smiles and "May I help you, sir" as if he was going to slobber on Stanley's pants. Stanley didn't know whether he should talk to this guy or not. Then Stanley figured, What the hell, what else am I supposed to do? Decent people have to buy underwear. *So he told the salesman in a low voice, casual-like, "I'm here to buy underwear." The salesman was thrilled, his face lighting up like it was someone's birthday.*

"Very good, sir. We have just what you need. What size will you be looking for?"

Stanley wanted the medium underwear. Stanley was a very medium sort of person in taste, habit, and dress.

"What color, sir?"

"White, please." Stanley wore white underwear. He suspected that swingers wore those other colors.

"Very good, sir. Will you want boxers or briefs or perhaps," the clerk giggled demurely, "boxer briefs?"

"Boxer briefs? What on earth are those?"

"Let me show you, sir. Right this way. We also have them in grey. What about long underwear? You'll be warm in a cold snap with those, sir. It's just dreadful to have cold knees. Sometimes you'd think your knees might freeze, it gets so cold even sitting around the house."

Stanley conceded that he might have a point.

"What about a thermal shirt? The waffle weave holds tiny pockets of warm air. Say you're at a football game, sitting outside on one of those cold seats. A full suit of thermal underwear would be just the thing. And how about a union suit? This style not only has the necessary opening in the seat for the bodily functions but a built-in truss, should you ever need it. If you'll just step this way to the fitting room, I'd like to show you a few more things I think would be just right for you." The heap of garments rose in Stanley's arms. "You may not think it would be practical, but this short kimono looks well over any pajamas. We also have over-the-calf socks, tube socks, bikini briefs, g-strings, girdles, and athletic supporters."

By this time, Stanley was completely buried in underwear. He couldn't lower his arms to reach his wallet. He couldn't find the three-way mirror, the sales counter or his fly. Soon he felt himself disappear outright beneath a mass of cotton knit. He simply ceased to exist entirely. At the end of the day, his car was impounded. After a month, the neighbors gave away his dog.

Randall's monologue was a surprise hit. At the end of the night, even the people who didn't especially like the piece had something nice to say, and Randall, a little shy at first, had fun with the feedback. As the crowd started to break up, Gustavo came over and congratulated him.

"Randall, that was amazing. Thank you so much for reading tonight."

"You're very welcome. I'm glad to know my story pleased, though maybe the cute boy over there didn't like it much. He seems to have fallen asleep."

Jason had found one of Lacey's sturdy wooden library armchairs in a corner by the children's books and made himself as comfortable as he could. He was turned to one side with his arm curled protectively around his computer bag. His eyes were closed. His shirttail was hanging out.

"Ha—that's my boyfriend, Jason. He's had a long day."

"Excuse me, I didn't know he was your boyfriend. I hope I didn't say anything offensive."

"You didn't. He's adorable, isn't he?"

Orion approached with his entourage to give his compliments to Gustavo, who had read something good of his own.

"Gustavo, your poem was incredible, as always."

"Thank you. Everyone did a great job. And this guy..." Gustavo turned toward Randall, grinning, "This guy is my classmate. I asked him if he'd like to read tonight because he did a great reading of a Sal Mariano poem. I had no idea he'd write something like that."

Orion looked at Randall as though he'd suddenly noticed him. "Oh yeah, you had the one about underwear. That was sort of interesting too."

Randall replied drily that it was very gracious of Orion to say so.

"Okay, well, we should get going," Orion said. "It was a wonderful evening. Thanks so much!" And with boys in tow, Orion took off.

After he left, Randall said, "'That was sort of interesting'? What a douchebag."

"Yeah, that was pretty douche-y."

"Who was that guy?"

"His name's Orion. He's a well-known local artist who likes to play mentor with younger guys he wants to bone."

"He was clearly impressed with *me*."

"Yeah, that was weird he didn't dig your piece. I dunno. Maybe it's because you're taller than he is. I don't think he likes looking up to people."

Randall laughed, then offered Gustavo and Jason a ride home.

"That would be nice. Thank you."

8

"WHAT ARE YOU DOING RIGHT NOW?" Randall had called Adam. It was Saturday morning, and Adam was drinking coffee and watching cartoons.

"Nothing much, just screwing off."

"I didn't interrupt you masturbating, did I?"

"Yes, I was masturbating, but I don't mind being interrupted."

"Masturbation is very beneficial," Randall said. "Did you know you should masturbate several times a day for prostate health?"

"Oh, good. I'm right on schedule."

"I called to ask if you want to go to the main library with me."

"Yeah, sure. Really I'm just sitting here having a second cup of coffee in front of the TV."

"Coffee is also good for your prostate."

"What can I say? I'm a prostate champion. What's at the library?"

"Not sure. But I'm hoping to find out more about Sal Mariano."

. . .

Randall drove down the ramp to the parking garage below Civic Center Plaza. "There's a big space just south of us on the other side of that wall. It used to be a convention center, but now it's used for storage."

"That's too bad," said Adam. "Why didn't it work out?"

"Ultimately, I think nobody really wanted it because it had a major case of the uglies. It's this windowless bunker with a bunch of block-shaped pilasters all over the place holding up the ceiling, similar to this garage. I dunno, I always sort of liked it."

When they climbed the stairs to the street, they were looking at the Asian Art Museum and the main public library.

"The library used to be in the building the Asian Art Museum is in now." Randall pointed from one to the other. "Before 1906, this site was the old city hall. Before that, it was a Gold Rush cemetery. When they were turning the old library into the museum, they found a bunch of graves that had never been moved when they built the old city hall. Apparently, they weren't that particular about it."

"Sounds like corpse relocation was too big an operation in those days to sweat the small stuff."

"You may be right about that. Weirdest of all, though, was when the foundation for the new library was being excavated, there was what looked like the outline of a ship."

"A ship?"

"Yeah. Ships are buried all along the waterfront in places where they filled in parts of the coast. By scuttling a ship, you could stake a land claim in that spot. But as you can see, we're nowhere near the water. And I don't remember hearing any explanation of what a ship might've been doing there. I've tried to find out more about it since, but nobody seems to know anything. But I remember being down here as a kid when they were digging the hole for the new building. I saw the shape of a hull in the sand."

As they walked toward the library, Adam asked, "So did you read something at that open mic?"

"Yeah, I did. Sorry I didn't invite you to be there but frankly, I was afraid I'd bomb."

"No worries. I get it. But it sounds like maybe you didn't bomb?"

Randall smirked. "Actually, I did pretty well. They liked it."

"Nice. And you knew about the open mic because of a guy from the seminar?"

"Yeah. I agreed to do it because he's really hot, and I would've agreed to anything that might've led to getting into his pants. He's a flirt too, but he has a boyfriend."

"Maybe the boyfriend doesn't care if he fools around?"

"Hm... maybe. And the boyfriend is cute."

Inside the library, Randall went over to one of the computers on a glass table and tried a few keywords.

"Where do we start?" asked Adam.

"I think we want some sort of government death index, but I don't really know what I'm looking for." He scrolled down a page. "Wait—maybe I found it: *California Death Index*. Fifth floor."

The records turned out to be on microfiche. They got help from a librarian who set them up with a projector and a card file of small sheets of blue-violet plastic. The records only went up to 1995. Randall had wondered if he would have to know the exact year of death, but groups of years were imaged together, so the boys didn't need to look through everything. They checked the most logical date ranges plus another couple just to be sure. Sal Mariano wasn't there, but there was still a whole decade the box didn't show.

"So he didn't die in California before 1996," Adam said.

"There's gotta be something else."

They went off to find the librarian again, who suggested they simply try the phone book. Sal wasn't in the most recent one, so they spot-checked a few older ones. That turned up nothing. Next to the telephone directories were enormous, hardbound volumes of something called *City Directory*, which contained addresses for virtually every person and business in San Francisco. Those stopped at 1982. "Each of these books must weigh as much as a headstone," said Randall.

"A tome-stone."

They hoisted up the last volume, spread it on a table, and sat down. They took a moment to work out how the book was organized, but soon they were leafing through the names.

"Well, what do you know?" Randall paused and stared at a page. "He's listed, or at least we could have a match on the name."

"Do you think the address might still be good?"

"We could try ringing the doorbell," Randall said, "though somehow that's weirder to me than a séance."

A little later, Randall and Adam sat a vegetarian restaurant nearby, mulling over their morning between bites of the curry of the day. The servers wore either a sari or a blue polo shirt and white pants, according to gender. Adam was impressed with the huge variety of people that filled the dining room.

"This is a cool, funky place."

"There's really nothing else quite like it in town," Randall said.

"So are we gonna check out Sal's address from 1982?"

"Maybe we could at least look at the building. I sort of feel like we have to, though I'm a little too nervous to knock on the door. What would we say?"

"Would it help if we took his poems to autograph in case he opens the door? If it's some random stranger, we could always say we were just autograph hunting."

"Maybe so. I dunno, maybe I should just write to his publisher. I don't think he's a hot seller these days but the check must go somewhere," Randall reasoned. "By the way, I meant to ask how things went with Eugene and that guy."

"Cody? They've seen each other since. He's an opera singer."

"Really? Somehow I wouldn't have imagined that."

"Yeah, me neither, but what do I know about opera? Anyway, he seems like a good guy, though I think he likes the night life a little more than Eugene. Well, almost anyone likes the night life more than Eugene."

Randall smiled. "Eugene seems just kind of... together."

"Yeah. That's a good word for him."

Eugene arrived at the bar on Folsom at a little after nine p.m., finding Cody sitting next to one of the guys who had been with him on the lawn the day they first met. When Eugene went over to them, Cody just said, "Hey, Eugene. Maybe you remember Ray."

The whole thing was very casual. Eugene told Cody again what a great concert it had been and how much he enjoyed hearing him sing. Ray hadn't been there, but he had wanted to come. He agreed Cody was an amazing singer. Eugene smiled at Ray, who gave a weak smile back.

Cody and Ray had ordered vodka and some kind of energy drink, which they admitted tasted nasty but kept drinking anyway. It sounded noxious. Eugene ordered beer.

An action movie played muted on the TV screens to the music from the sound system. It was just possible to follow what was going on. Eugene didn't usually go for that kind of entertainment but had trouble not watching it. Ray started text messaging with some other guys, who wanted to meet at a different bar. Cody went to the restroom. Eugene watched the movie and made funny small talk about it to Ray, who was polite but cagey. Cody came back. By then, the other guys had changed their minds and were going to some dude's apartment on Market in the Castro. So Eugene, Cody, and Ray finished their drinks and found a cab. Cody rode in the middle.

The apartment on Market was a sparse studio with a sofa on one side under the window and bed on the other. There was porn on the TV while trance came out of the speakers on each side of the computer. Their host was a good-looking guy about thirty in sweats and a nylon shirt with an athletic gear logo. The other two dudes had already arrived.

The room was lit by screens and one lamp next to the bed. The Venetian blinds let in broken glimpses of city light. Eugene talked a little with the other boys. There was some good weed. There was also a red sports drink Eugene declined. He got to know Ray a little better. They all talked about how much they liked the porn. Ray was checking out Eugene's body. Cody didn't seem to mind if Eugene and Ray kissed.

After a while, they were going to head over to some other dude's place near Alamo Square. They were too many for one cab. Someone wanted something at the store. Eugene, Cody, and Ray waited a bit while the others went ahead. A cab showed up and took them to an apartment with high ceilings on the first floor of a Victorian. Batik bedspread, more porn. The host had on some chill-out music, and they chilled.

The next morning at the gym, Steve showed up for his training session and Eugene was a little bleary.

"Sorry—I'm kinda low-energy today. I was out with Cody all night."

"I hope you had a good time."

Eugene thought for a moment, then said, "I dunno what, exactly, I had."

9

MONDAY MORNING. On the left side of the lobby in the main CUE building was a lounge with a few chairs, a bulletin board, and some shelves for flyers and other print media. Adam picked up a movie house calendar before heading down the corridor with his coffee to the MFA office. He greeted Delma and spread the calendar on his desk. Delma peered over her reading glasses.

"That looks like the Castro Theatre calendar. Anything good?"

There was a small Humphrey Bogart festival that week. Adam had noticed it on the marquee as he was walking along Castro on Sunday. The general object of his quest was one of his family's favorites, *The Maltese Falcon*, but he was open to other ideas. "It would be nice to see something I don't know, but mostly I just want to go to something at the Castro. I want a big screen experience."

Delma, a crime fiction buff, came over to offer suggestions. She pointed to *Dark Passage*. "You should try to get to that one if you're interested in the City." Tapping her index finger on *The Big Sleep*, she said, "That one's fun, if convoluted." She went through *Casablanca, Treasure of the Sierra Madre, To Have and Have Not*, and *Key Largo*.

Ted came in.

"Hey Ted," said Delma. "Which one of these Bogart films should Adam see besides *The Maltese Falcon*?"

"Only one?" Ted went over to look. "I dunno—maybe *Dark Passage*? There's lots of good San Francisco in that."

"That's what *I* said," Delma noted with satisfaction.

Ted asked Adam for enrollment figures for all MFA students in all courses for the last five years. He had a meeting in two days with the senior administration about the department's budget. Ted would need to put off the student services manager hire a little while longer, which might've been working against him, but it would be just as bad to have to onboard someone right now as it was to do without. And besides, Adam had turned out to be a surprisingly good addition.

A little later while Literature of the Counterculture was taking a fifteen minute break, Randall went to talk to Gustavo.

"Hello there. I see you're looking well."

"Thanks, you too," said Gustavo. "How's it going?"

"Not too bad. I've been indulging in a little research project you might find interesting. Have you ever wondered what happened to Sal Mariano?"

"Hm... I've never really thought about it. He doesn't seem to have been one of the ones to die of something self-inflicted. Is he still alive?"

"A very good question," said Randall. "I haven't been able to find out. I think he probably is, but I'm not sure. He may have just faded into obscurity."

"Maybe Ellen knows?"

"She didn't offhand, but she was intrigued by the question

too. She's going to ask some friends of hers who know people who would have known him. In the meantime, I'm going to write to his publisher."

"That's a good idea. I'm sure they'd have to know."

"Exactly. Maybe Sal's not the most famous Beat writer, but someone somewhere would need to collect whatever royalties there might be. I probably shouldn't admit this, but I went to the library for a little analog stalking and found an old street address from 1982."

"Wow! Are you gonna check it out?"

"I was thinking of at least driving by. I feel a little creepy doing that but the listing was twenty-three years old. In all likelihood, he's moved on. And it could have been a different Salvatore Mariano, for all I know. Still, it would be nice to see the house and imagine him living there."

"Well, if you do, let me know what you find."

As Adam was getting ready to leave the office for the day, he announced to Delma and Ted he was going explore the city on his own without any sort of plan, going wherever the mood struck him. He shut down his computer and wandered out of the building, heading vaguely north and west. The past few weeks had been filled with adventure but rarely alone. The city was all the noisier, busier, more frenetic in the evening rush, but the balmy summer air gave everything wings. He rambled through the streets till he found a bar with rock music flowing from the door. The place advertised a patio. He went in, ordered a pint, and found a seat outside.

Then he looked over at a table full of people and saw Oliver among them. Oliver had not yet seen him. Adam sipped his pint. Eventually, Oliver would notice him. Adam could do nothing about that except leave, but he stayed put. It was a nice evening. The music was good. There was plenty of room on the patio if Oliver wanted to avoid him.

After about fifteen minutes, a young woman at Oliver's table got up to go. They had started breaking up for the night. Adam looked over and just then, Oliver met his gaze. Adam gave a polite nod. Oliver nodded back. When two more people got up to go, Oliver picked up his backpack, said something to his companions, and walked over to Adam. His fair skin looked almost translucent in the grey shade of the patio.

"Hi," said Oliver, a little hesitant. "Thanks for your note."

"Sorry for the trouble."

"You seem like a nice guy."

"So do you. Would you like to sit down?" said Adam. "I promise to behave."

Oliver smiled. "Sometimes I'm also an uptight guy."

"A little miscommunication. I don't normally talk that way to people I just met unless I'm pretty sure they'll like it."

Oliver nodded. "Are you here by yourself?"

"Yeah, I just finished work and decided to check out the city a little."

"I just got done with work too. My coworkers and I sometimes come here cause it's close by." Oliver's voice was quiet but not too low to hear over the music.

"Grateful Peas looks like a nice store. Do you like working there?"

"Not all that much but it's okay for a summer job. The customers can be annoying, and except for the people I was just with, my coworkers aren't all that friendly."

"That's too bad. My job is pretty boring," Adam said, "but at least the people are nice. And I like the vibe in our department."

"You work at College for the Urban Environment?"

"Yeah, in the MFA office."

"That sounds interesting."

Adam laughed. "It's not. Don't get me wrong. The school is great. It's like a holdover from the '60s—totally the San Francisco I had been dreaming about. I'd love to be a student there. And the office manager is really cool, and I like the director of the department a lot. But my job is to help out with these big, hairy-scary reports for the central administration and clean up the department's records and stuff. So the actual work isn't all that exciting."

"How long are you in San Francisco for?"

"My sublet is over at the end of September."

"And then you go back to Brooklyn?"

"Yeah, that's the plan." Adam paused for a moment. "Are you originally from San Francisco?"

"I grew up in Oakland. I'm living there now with my family, trying to save money. I'm starting a doctoral program in plant biology this fall."

"That sounds cool. I wish I was that focused. One of the reasons I came to San Francisco for the summer, other than getting this incredible sublet, was to get away from thinking about reality for a little while. I always thought this would be an amazing place but never imagined actually coming here somehow—probably because it's not the sort of thing I could've believed myself doing."

"I've heard people say the Bay Area's on their list of places to go but don't really think of it that way because I don't know what it's like to live anywhere else."

"You're lucky," said Adam. "New York is a special place too, but it's not like here." Adam looked at Oliver's grey eyes, his copper-gold eyebrows and pale eyelashes. He was an intense, awkward guy, but he was starting to open up a bit. Adam asked him if he'd like another beer. "I'm not trying to come on to you or anything, I swear."

Oliver laughed. "I shouldn't have another because I have to get on a bicycle."

"You take BART to get home?"

"Yeah."

"Well, what about… maybe this is kind of sudden to be asking you this, and I hope you don't think I'm out of line, but would you have that beer with me on Thursday, then go to a showing of a Humphrey Bogart movie at the Castro Theatre? No expectations, I promise. I was planning to go by myself anyway."

"I've never seen a Humphrey Bogart movie," Oliver said.

"Then you'll go with me?" Adam started to get excited. "No funny stuff, I swear. I'll be good the whole time."

When he told Eugene later, Adam could barely believe it himself. "He actually said yes."

"You sound like you wish he hadn't."

"It's not that—it's just that I got all geeked out about the movie and didn't stop to think it might be weird if this serious, brainy guy I offended by accident would actually go with me. Now I don't know what I'm gonna do with him. What'll we talk about?"

"You don't have to say much—you're going to a movie."

10

THURSDAY, lunchtime. Jason bought a deli sandwich and took it to Yerba Buena Gardens. He sat down on a bench near the waterfall and carefully unwrapped the extra outer paper to get to the two halves, which were still partly connected by the inner wrapper that wasn't cut through on one side. As soon as he had eaten one half, he got up, exposed a corner of the other, holding the brown bag around it, and munched while strolling and looking at the public art all around him, the posters for Yerba Buena Center, and the museum across the street.

Duane was about to cross the street at Howard and 3rd, attempting to degrease his fingers from the eggroll he had just scarfed. He was headed toward the park to shoot some photos on his lunch break, and he didn't want to get any oil on the camera or the body of the lens. He had gone through the supply of paper napkins from the Chinese restaurant, which blotted away what he could see, then he scrubbed his fingertips on the denim of his pants for good measure.

After finishing his sandwich, Jason still had a few precious minutes before he needed to start walking back. So he half-sat, half-leaned on a low wall and watched the people. Some were going to and from work, cutting through the park for a change of scene. Some relaxed on the grass, reading or eating. Some had bicycles next to them. Tourists looked all around, trying to make sense of where they were. Someone in a wheelchair was parked near a bench in the sun, face upturned to the light. A guy with a fancy camera was shooting candids of passersby. Jason watched this for a while. The guy with the camera was someone Jason had seen lately. He had been one of the visitors at that art opening for the photographer who had flirted with him and Gustavo. Jason watched the photographer more intently.

Duane was concentrating on what he was doing and didn't see Jason watching him until Jason happened to be in the frame of a shot. Duane suddenly noticed Jason looking back at him, and he smiled. He pointed to the camera and then to Jason and made a quizzical face. Jason smiled and nodded. After Duane clicked the shutter release a few times, he walked over to where Jason was perched.

"Hi there. Thanks for letting me take your photo. Would you like to see the pictures?"

"Yeah, sure."

Duane showed him the screen in the back of the camera.

"I think they came out well. I'd be happy to email these to you, if you'd like. I'm Duane, by the way."

"Nice to meet you, Duane. I'm Jason. Yeah, it would be great if you could send them to me. You must take great pictures since I don't mind the way I look in them."

Duane laughed. "You look great."

"Thanks. You must take a lot of pictures. That's a pretty impressive camera."

"I work in a camera store," Duane said with a shrug.

Jason dug in a pocket for his wallet and found a business card.

"You can send the photos to that address. I wouldn't mind looking at more of your pictures. Do you have a website?"

"You mean like for photography? I hadn't thought about putting anything on the internet, though I don't know why not."

That evening, Adam rode the 33 bus from work to the Castro to meet Oliver at the theater. Oliver was waiting near the curb in front of the marquee, standing with his backpack and bicycle helmet, a little hippy-ish. Adam waved.

Oliver waved back and smiled. He had never been to a movie with a guy before. Or rather, he had been to a movie with a whole bunch of friends all at once and some of them were guys. Adam was really confident. He was also nice. A nice, confident guy had asked Oliver out to a movie. That never happened.

"Are you hungry?" Adam asked. "We could get something fast before it starts."

"Yeah, that would be good."

"There's a pizzeria over there, or... do you eat pizza?" Adam laughed. "Sorry, that sounded a little odd. I just wondered, since you work in an organic grocery store if you eat that kind of thing."

"Yeah," Oliver said with a smile. "Pizza's fine."

They went to the place across the street. Adam decided on a slice of pepperoni and mushroom. Oliver got mushroom and tomato. The pizzeria had beer too. They found a couple of seats along the wall.

Adam's slice had been out of the oven exactly the right amount of time, and he wolfed it down. "Sorry," he said between bites. "No one should have to watch me eat."

That got a laugh out of Oliver, at least. It was hard to tell if Adam was getting anywhere at all. There was a lot of quiet to Oliver. Adam talked enough for the two of them, explaining how his friends at work recommended this movie because it had been filmed in San Francisco, telling Oliver about Humphrey Bogart, *The Maltese Falcon*, and Dashiell Hammett, and how excited Adam was to see a movie like *Dark Passage* in a real theater.

"Sorry, I'm running off at the mouth."

"It's okay," said Oliver, looking at Adam's honest brown eyes. "It's interesting. And I know I'm really awkward sometimes."

"Man, I'm glad you said that. I was nervous that it was just me. Wait, sorry, I mean, not that I thought you were awkward but—I should just stop talking already."

Oliver laughed again. "Don't worry. Sometimes I don't talk enough."

"I'm the exact opposite of that right now."

"It's all right. I like your Brooklyn accent."

"Really?"

"Yeah. It's nice."

It was Adam's turn to be quiet.

Oliver said, "So what's life like in Brooklyn?"

"It's okay, or at least my neighborhood's a pretty nice place to live. It's not exciting or fashionable, but it's comfortable. I never thought about it much when I was going to school. Then I found out from my older brother about a sublet here. Maybe this sounds clueless, but it dawned on me that, yeah, maybe I could go somewhere else besides Manhattan or something. So I asked my best friend Eugene if he'd come with me, and we just went for it."

"It sounds really exciting."

"It is. More than I thought I would be. People keep saying it's the kind of place you don't want to leave, and I'm beginning to see why."

Adam asked how Oliver's day went.

"It was fine, I guess. Not much happened. Work was kind of boring."

"Yeah, same here. I was mostly just looking forward to this."

"Yeah, me too."

When Oliver had finished eating, they went out to the sidewalk.

"Is your bike locked up somewhere nearby?"

"Yeah, over there," Oliver gestured in the direction of a bike rack.

They crossed to the theater and bought their tickets. While Oliver went to the restroom, Adam checked out the lobby. A tall window with an ornate grille let in the early evening light. The concession stand served espresso drinks, something he hadn't seen in a movie house before. When Oliver returned, they went inside to find some seats. The auditorium was even grander than it looked in photos. The walls were decorated with murals framed by gilt pilasters, and the equally ornate ceiling seemed to be covered with leather.

When the seats were mostly full, the lights dimmed, and a massive theater organ console rose to the height of the curtain with a fanfare. As the organist played a selection of popular songs from the 1930s and '40s, Adam noticed Oliver studying him.

"You're looking at me," Adam said in a low voice, smiling nervously. "Did I mess up again?"

"No, sorry, it's nothing bad. I just—sorry, I'm weird."

Several blocks away, the League of Lavender Engineers gathered again for another pleasant evening in Richard and Chuck's Eureka Valley aerie. The summer evening light over the city was transformed by the incoming fog. Richard took a quick photo before pouring Chardonnay for the guests. ("Anderson Valley?" "Carneros.") The aroma from the kitchen mingled with the smell of a new tribal rug. Chuck's appetizers were delicious.

Everyone talked about much they enjoyed the barbecue at Aaron and Jeff's on the Fourth. Aaron and Jeff were very nearly done with renovations in the master bath and talked of building a brick oven in the garden. Chuck said that if they did, he wanted some of the bread. Everyone loved what Aaron and Jeff had done with the house. Mark and Kyle talked about wanting more outdoor space, and how they were thinking about moving to a bigger house. Maybe they'd get a dog. Another couple they all knew just got one of those dogs you saw everywhere at the moment. What was that kind of dog? Were there trends in dogs? Richard said there were trends in everything.

Richard and Chuck were going to hike Shasta. Jeff and Aaron were thinking about a camping getaway to Manresa Beach. They really wanted to go on a cruise to Finland, but that would wait till the house wasn't tying up so much of their cash-flow. Kyle, the youngest in the group, if only by a few years, wondered if those gay cruises were boring. After all, weren't cruises in general sort of boring? Richard, one of the oldest, said that some were and some weren't.

Mark and Kyle had gone to a classical concert at the conservatory with some other people they knew. They had liked the music but forgot about all that when a handsome young baritone came onstage, Cody Gallagher. Chuck knew all about him and said he was a hunk. But more lean and boyish, Mark thought. That could possibly be a hunk too, Chuck argued. There was a general discussion of hunkiness. Richard asked what the lean, boyish hunk had sung, but Mark and Kyle couldn't remember. Whatever it was, it had been really beautiful. Chuck went to check on the food.

The sky had gone dark, and the fog had descended from Twin Peaks and Mount Sutro. On Castro Street, the crowd flowed out of movie theater onto the tile-bordered sidewalk in front of the ticket box. When Oliver said that he had really enjoyed it, Adam was over the moon, but he started coming to earth fast because the time was getting late.

"You probably have to head over to BART soon," Adam said, "but would you like to walk around a little?"

"I don't need to go right away. I can hang out for a while."

Turning south, they made their way toward 18th Street and the steep streets of Eureka Valley to the west.

"Did you recognize any of the places in the movie?" Adam asked.

"Not really," said Oliver with an apologetic smile. "I should spend more time on this side of the Bay."

"You could come over here for something besides work."

"Maybe I could."

After a couple of blocks, there were only a few shops among the residential buildings, and soon they didn't even see a corner store. The boys wandered among gingerbread cottages, passing windows that glowed with the warmth of comfort and content-ment. They wanted to explore a grassy hillside open space, but the path looked too difficult in the dark. They rambled the villagelike streets till they were on the upper part of Market. At that altitude, the architecture became boxy, but the steep hill-side and the glow of electric light turned the plainest apart-ment houses into castles. Neither of the boys knew the neighborhood. Adam didn't know exactly when Oliver had to be back, but Oliver didn't seem worried about it. Adam didn't ask.

Wandering down a cul-de-sac, they at last found an upper entrance to the hillside park they saw earlier and stepped onto the turf, looking out over the city. The wind was cold and damp.

They stood in silence for a while until Adam said, "Whatcha thinking, Mr. Oliver?"

Oliver looked at him, doing that quiet thing again that was hard to read, except he seemed to want to be there. He was smiling. It was a funny sort of self-conscious smile, but a smile nonetheless. Maybe he even knew that they were on a date, and that he was enjoying it.

Oliver said, "I'm thinking that it's really beautiful up here. I'm glad we did this."

"So am I. I'm glad you came out with me tonight."

As they stood looking out at the lights and the fog, Adam said, "You're really handsome, Mr. Oliver."

"Thanks," said Oliver, then added a little later than ideal, "you are too."

Adam laughed.

Oliver laughed too. "Sorry—that didn't come out the way I meant it to."

"It's okay. I could tell."

"I don't do this very often."

"That's okay too. Can I ask you something, Mr. Oliver?"

"Sure."

"Would you go out with me again?"

"Yes. I would."

"All right. Then it's a date."

11

"Hey Adam, how's it hanging?" Randall was on the phone. It was Sunday morning.

"Very well. Thank you for asking."

"Listen, I called to see if you'd like to go on a short Beat Writer tour."

"Yeah, sounds great. But there's something I want to talk about first."

"Oh? Do tell."

Adam explained that he had taken time to apologize to Oliver, and it had led to a date, a pretty good one. They might see each other again. Adam didn't know how Randall would feel about that.

"I'd be kidding if I said I wasn't at all envious," said Randall, "but I think people should be free to be happy."

"Thanks. You're a prince."

"Might you still be up for getting naked sometime?"

"Yeah, sure, though maybe not right this second."

"Very good. Can I interest you in taking a ride around town with me instead?"

An hour later, they were in the van, headed northeast. Adam asked where they were going.

"First stop, 710 Montgomery, former address of the Black Cat Café. It had been both a Beat Generation landmark and a gay landmark."

"More Sal Mariano?"

"Correct."

When they got to the one-time home of the Black Cat, it was very, very gone, having served its last drink over forty years before. Adam asked what had happened to it.

"Unfortunately," explained Randall, "there was a rabidly homophobic state law aimed at gay bars. The idea was to have the cops shut down any establishment where 'perverts' were congregating. The owner of the Black Cat and the Widow Norton fought back for years, but the legal fees were overwhelming, and they closed in '64."

"That's fucked up," said Adam.

"Yes, yes it is."

The boys drove on. Randall pointed out former apartments and hangouts of writers, painters, and musicians. Carefully negotiating the crossing of Columbus at Stockton, he turned onto Green. "Over there under Caffè Sport used to be a jazz and poetry venue called The Cellar." There was too much to take in at once in this intensely alive part of town. They turned onto Grant Avenue. Randall indicated a nondescript storefront on the right. "That place was... The Place, one of the great open mic spots of the era."

"Too bad you missed it, Randall," said Adam.

"Indeed," Randall concurred. "Holy frijoles—a parking spot." He expertly swung the van around at Filbert Street. "Can I interest you in a cappuccino?"

They walked up Grant to the Caffè Trieste.

. . .

"It's hard to tell what he's thinking." Adam sipped carefully at the foam on his coffee.

"Yes," Randall said, "I know what you mean."

"He's also got some of the prettiest coloring I've ever seen."

"That hair is really something," said Randall.

"And his eyes are like rain."

"So may I ask if you scored a home run?"

"I didn't even get to first base. And that was more than okay. I never hoped to. At first, I wasn't even sure he liked me at all. After the movie, we went for a walk and got a little lost, but we found this park on a hill with a view. It was cold and windy, but somehow that was part of it too."

"It sounds really nice," Randall said.

"It was."

They sat quietly for a moment, then Adam asked where they were headed next.

"I'm thinking I could just quickly point out a few more things over here, then drive by Sal Mariano's last known address. After that, I'll drop you wherever you want."

"Where is this place?"

"Lone Mountain."

Randall took Broadway most of the way. There was a tunnel right in the middle of a heavily residential neighborhood where Adam was least expecting it.

"They built this after the war to move traffic more efficiently," said Randall. "Another one of the city's can-do projects."

They turned south at Divisadero and drove around the base of Lone Mountain, which turned out to be more of a hill, toward the western slope. Passing the ornate spires of USF, they entered a side street with a row of small, jewel-like Victorian houses. Randall stopped in front of one, and they looked for a while.

"Do you think he's in there?" asked Adam.

"I dunno," Randall replied. "Even if he isn't, I already feel like I'm stalking."

"He lived here in 1982, right? That's a pretty long time ago."

They stared at the house for a moment longer, then Randall started the engine again.

"This is a great space!" Duane looked around at what had been the living room and the dining room in the original layout of the apartment, now filled with Seth's books, photo equipment, and bedroom furniture. The two rooms were at the back of the building, away from the street, and connected by a pair of pocket doors. Large bay windows let in plenty of light from garden. On the opposite side of one of the rooms was a closet door that could be hidden with backdrop paper, which hung on a roll from the ceiling. In the adjacent room, which had been made darker, was a full-sized bed, a dresser, and a work table.

"Ugh, it's a hovel," said Seth. He pulled down a length of white background paper.

"Should I take off my clothes?"

"It's up to you. Well, maybe your shirt for now," Seth said, setting up a tripod. Duane took off his flannel shirt and t-shirt and threw them on the bed. Seth turned on some lights. "You have a really nice natural body."

"Thanks. It's not worked out like yours, though. Your body is great."

"Sometimes natural is better. Some people really go for natural."

"What would you like me to do?"

"Um... just stand there for a second."

Duane stood there, looking around the room. "I love that black and white photo of the dude on the fire escape."

"Thanks. I took that on a trip to New York. You look really

good in this light. You make a good model. You should do commercial modeling."

Duane was looking at the camera. Seth tried a few shots.

"You mean like for ads and stuff? I dunno. I hadn't really thought about it. I'm not sure I'm tall enough to be a model."

"It's not like runway modeling. You can be any type as long as you're photogenic. Try turning your body toward the door but keep your head where it is. Yeah, that's good."

Seth brought over the chair from the work table and had Duane sit in it in various poses.

"I can't believe Hengist is closing," Seth said.

"I know. I wish I could do something. I wish I could buy it."

"What really pisses me off is that it's another fucking thing gone. Another thing that made San Francisco special. This town is turning into a corporate yuppie hell."

Seth's verdict seemed to hang over the whole room so Duane sat quietly and made his face a blank.

After a while, he said to Seth, "How do you sell your art? I need to figure out how to sell my stuff, but I don't really know where to begin."

"It's not hard to find ways to sell your art."

That sounded simple but didn't help much.

"Make what you make," said Seth. "Just keep making it and people will buy it. What kind of art do you make?

Duane made objects, paintings, photos, and, occasionally, furniture.

"Make one thing. Even if it's in different forms, make one thing."

The thing that Duane made kept changing.

"Well, you're really natural and sexy. Make something like that."

"I have trouble seeing myself."

"You'll figure it out."

Duane hesitated for a moment.

"I don't really know myself sexually."

"Try taking off your pants," said Seth, who was framing a shot. "Wait, that came out wrong."

Early evening in Hayes Valley. Eugene stood in front of Steve and Hector's first floor apartment with a few groceries in a bag and rang the bell. Steve opened the door.

"Hey! You found us! Good to see you!"

"I brought some veggies and other ingredients."

Hector came in from the next room and they made introductions.

"You fellas ready to make some food?" Eugene asked.

"We're always ready to make food," said Hector.

They went to the kitchen to unpack the bag. A large, orange cat hopped up on the counter. Hector grabbed him and put him back on the floor.

"Sorry—this is Sam."

Eugene scratched Sam behind his left ear. "Hello Sam. Would you like to help us cook?"

"Sam is an expert," said Steve. "His main ingredient is cat hair."

They pulled some more items from the fridge and the cupboard. Eugene washed, prepped, and kept clearing things away while guiding his hosts through most of the actual cooking.

"After we eat," said Steve, "I'd like to show you something to try on. No pressure."

"Uh-oh," said Eugene with a smile.

Hector laughed. "It's a spandex suit we got for a superhero-themed movie. We were wondering if you might be willing to model it for us. It's okay if you don't want to, but it should fit you, and we want to see how it looks on a real, live body."

. . .

Dinner was a success, and they all overate. "Mostly vegetables," said Eugene with a grin. Later on, Hector cleared the table while Steve sat with Eugene in the living room to check out the suit, which was red and silver grey.

"It has a fly!" Eugene said, laughing.

"We made sure to order the crotch zipper," said Hector, standing in the doorway. "You'd obviously want to have that feature anyway..."

"But for a porn movie, that would be pretty important," said Eugene, finishing the thought. He was a little dubious but intrigued about the whole thing, and definitely amused to be asked.

"So would you model it for us?"

"Yeah, sure. Um, what should I do?"

"You can change in the bedroom," Steve told him. "And we're not asking you to make the movie. We just want to see how it looks on an actual superhero body."

"Oh man—you flatter me. After all we just ate." Eugene patted his belly. "I feel like a snake that swallowed a bowling ball."

Eugene went into the bedroom and emerged a couple of minutes later. The suit fit perfectly. Nobody said anything, but Eugene had decided that undies would spoil the effect.

"Wow!" said Hector.

"You look great in it," said Steve grinning. "How does it feel?"

"It's pretty comfortable. I don't think I'd want to sleep in it but it's no worse than a lot of athletic gear I've worn."

"It looks really good on you," said Hector. "Just so you know, you'd be welcome to make a movie."

Eugene gave his friends a crooked smile. "Hm... I'll keep that in mind."

12

JASON HAD JUST LEFT a beer bust after a fun day with Mike and Troy and James. Gustavo had needed to work but that was okay. While Gustavo was at the bookstore, Jason decided to run an errand at an art supply store on Market Street.

Inside were all kinds of beautiful and intimidating things Jason knew nothing about. The colors were especially exciting but Jason was going to start very basic, which seemed to mean a black pencil on inexpensive white paper. And an eraser. Especially the eraser. A cheerful woman with a flower painted on her cheekbone came over and asked if he'd like some help.

"I'm trying to learn how to draw," he said.

They looked at basic sketch pads, drawing pencils and pencil sharpeners, and, of course, erasers.

"You might not feel like you're ready for this," she said, "but I'd like to show you some pastel pencils."

He ended up buying a how-to book, some pencils in a few basic hardnesses, a brass sharpener, a 9x12 sketch pad, a pen-shaped eraser with smooth, white inserts, and some of the soft pastel pencils the salesperson suggested. He even allowed himself to get some different colors: an indigo, a crimson, and a forest green that reminded him somehow of Gustavo.

When he got home, he put the drawing book in the bottom of a drawer of personal documents. He started to put the art supplies into his laptop case, but he had time for one experiment before Gustavo got home.

Adam met Oliver outside Grateful Peas Grocery. Oliver was without his bike that day since they had decided to go check out some of the places in the movie they had seen.

"How do you wanna get there?" Adam asked.

"I dunno. I don't really where it is. Sorry—I'm not all that good with this part of the city."

"We'll figure it out."

When Adam had told Randall about their plans, he had suggested they start at Filbert and Sansome. A couple of buses went pretty near their destination, but waiting for one would take time, maybe longer than waiting for BART, which wouldn't take them as near but would be less plodding at rush hour.

"How do you feel about taking BART to Montgomery then walking the rest of the way?" Adam asked.

"I guess that would be okay. You know where we're going, right?"

"Roughly."

On the way to the station, Adam asked about Oliver's day.

"About like usual."

"About like usual, Mr. Oliver?" Adam was smiling and trying not to walk into people and other obstacles while admiring Oliver's serious, handsome face.

"Yeah, well, it's nicer now."

"My day is nicer now too. Much nicer. You ready for a little sightseeing?"

They went down into the station and rode BART to Montgomery Street. When they came up to street level again, they stood among Financial District skyscrapers.

"Which way?" asked Oliver.

"This is Montgomery. I think we wanna be a block to the east."

Oliver asked, "Is this what Midtown Manhattan is like?"

"Yeah, pretty much. Only there's a lot more of it."

North of the Transamerica Pyramid, the soaring towers gave way to smaller buildings. At Vallejo Street, the ground rose steeply to the west, but they kept going north where it was still fairly flat. As they crossed Green Street, the road to their left stopped abruptly at the foot of a steep, leafy incline: Telegraph Hill. Soon the sidewalk on the west side of the street ended. There was a parking lane with room to pass alongside the hill, which was reinforced with fencing. A long, black pipe came down through the brush, hugging the slope, and went into a bigger concrete pipe that went underground.

"I guess that's someone's sewer line," said Adam with a wry smile.

At Filbert, the road ended at a wall and a staircase, and they began a long ascent amid the greenery. The Bay Bridge floated in the early evening summer light. They paused often to look at the view and the variety of flowering plants all around them. Suddenly at Montgomery Street, they were beside a white and silver art deco apartment house they recognized from the movie.

"Wow, we made it," said Oliver.

"Did you think we wouldn't?"

"Well, I wasn't sure we'd find it."

Adam laughed and said, "I could tell we were going the right way."

"How did you know?"

"I dunno—it just looked like the right way. But would it have mattered if we had got lost?"

Oliver shrugged.

"Hey there, Oliver."

"Hey there, Adam."

The view shimmered in front of them as they stood looking out at the Bay. A few small, red-gold curls too short for Oliver's ponytail framed his face near his ears. Adam turned to look at him. They were standing close to each other.

"Oliver, would you like it if I held your hand?"

Oliver nodded.

Adam took Oliver's right hand in both of his own and examined it, holding it gently.

"I like hands."

Oliver watched as Adam explored his fingers, thumb, the soft place in the center of the palm. It was strangely intimate and frank, but Oliver didn't shy away. He looked at Adam's hands as well as they traced lines and folds. Then Adam gave him a light squeeze across the insides of the knuckles and released him. They continued up the steps, climbing past hanging gardens and houses that looked impossible to move furniture into, then paused below Coit Tower.

Adam turned toward the water again. "This is the most beautiful place on earth."

"Yes, it is," said Oliver, seeing his own side of the bay in the distance as he never had before.

"And climbing these stairs hurts with a boner."

Oliver tried not to laugh. "That was totally... unnecessary." He flushed pink, annoyed and amused, and annoyed by being amused.

"I'm sorry," said Adam with solemnity. "You're right, that was totally dumb and immature. I apologize."

They pretended to look at the scenery.

Adam said, "Hey Oliver, everything okay?"

"Yeah."

Adam took a step closer. "Good, cause I have something to say."

"What?"

"Boner."

"You're a dork."

As the boys went down the other side of Filbert into North Beach, the hills and valleys of the city took their breath away. Turning south at Grant Avenue, the sidewalks were alive with light and sound and people. They wandered the narrow street past bars and boutique windows to Green Street, where the smell of food was irresistible. Everything looked good. They picked the first restaurant they saw and went in. The server was a middle-aged woman who could tell they were on a date and liked them right away.

Adam studied the menu. "Do you know anything about wine?"

"Not really," Oliver said.

"Red or white?"

"Uh, red."

"My favorite flavor."

When their dinner order was in, Adam said, "What's your family like?"

"They're good people. I guess I'm really lucky to have them. My dad's quiet and a little distant, but he's a really gentle person. He's a biologist. My mom is a dietician. She's much more outgoing than my dad. I have a younger sister, Lilly. She just finished sophomore year. She's home for the summer. She's a little like my mom, more of an extrovert compared to me or my dad."

"Are you out to them?"

Oliver shrugged. "They know. It's too weird for me to talk about with them. But they're okay with it. I think they're more comfortable with it than I am with them knowing about it."

"I can understand that. Like it's too personal, maybe?"

"Yeah." Oliver almost squirmed. "What about your family? Do they know?"

"Yeah. They had a little trouble with it at first. Everybody knew about the gay people in the neighborhood, but we didn't talk about them openly, so when I told my parents, it was uncomfortable, like they didn't know what to do with it. But they seem okay with it now. Or if they're not, they don't say anything. Maybe it made it easier on them when Eugene and I became friends because they could see he wasn't gonna get me into trouble and he had my back. They love Eugene. They think he's better at life and more mature than me—probably because he is." Adam laughed. "Actually, I think it's more like Eugene is one of those people who sees a clear path ahead of him. Maybe you might be like that too."

"No, not at all," Oliver said, smiling. "I'm just guessing. Thinking about it too much is scary. I just know I have to do it somehow, so I sort of stumble forward."

The salads arrived, and the boys were hungry.

"This is really good," said Adam, trying not to show everything in his mouth while he talked. There were all kinds of vegetables and garbanzo and kidney beans. "I'm glad you got the same cause it has raw onion in it."

"It *is* good," Oliver agreed, munching. They ate in silence for a while. Then Oliver asked, "Do you have any siblings?"

"Yeah, a brother and two sisters, but they're all much older than me. Nobody put it exactly this way, but it's pretty clear I was a surprise, if you get what I mean."

Oliver laughed. "What do your parents do?"

"My dad's a pharmacist and my mom's a paralegal. They're sort of fun in a low-key way. They like movies and old rock records and the Mets. My dad was really excited I was going to San Francisco. He'd like to take a trip like this. I'm pretty sure my mother was a little anxious for me but tried not to let on. This is the farthest I've been away for a lengthy period of time without them. I lived at home for college. This is the first time I've stepped out on my own."

After dinner, they walked around the neighborhood and bought some Italian cookies in a bakery so they could take them to the park.

"Have you ever had a boyfriend?" Adam asked.

Oliver shook his head. "There were a few guys I tried dating but nothing ended up going anywhere. I think I was too uptight for one of them. There was another guy who was nice but really boring and even more awkward than I am. How about you? Have you ever had a boyfriend?"

"Not real relationships—just some regular buddies I get together with. I like those fellas okay, but nothing serious." Studying Oliver's face, Adam said, "Uh-oh. Suddenly you're looking at me like maybe I'm a total creep."

"No, it's just—I wish I could... I just get weird about stuff sometimes. Part of me would like to explore more. But then I start to go into a kind of low-grade panic when I think of all the things that could go wrong and all the things I could catch. Any of that would be more than I could deal with, so I just avoid a lot of situations. But it gets in the way of meeting guys."

"That's a shame, Mr. Oliver."

"I know."

As they made their way down Columbus toward Montgomery Station, Adam said, "You probably have to head back to Oakland, huh?"

"I can stay longer. I don't have to work tomorrow."

"I do, but we don't have to be up too late. We could hang out at my place for a while. But it's pretty far from BART."

"We could get a cab."

"You'd like come home with me?"

"Yes, I would."

They were at the base of the Pyramid at Montgomery.

"You could even stay the night, if it got too late."

"I could."

"Will your folks wonder where you are?"

"I can let them know."

At California Street, they found a cab.

They had slept very lightly, so Adam had no trouble waking up in time for work, but he didn't want to go. He wanted to spend the rest of the morning with his arm over Oliver, looking at his red-gold curls on the pillow.

"Hey, Oliver. You awake?"

"Yeah."

Adam squeezed him tight.

"Guess I better get moving," Adam murmured against Oliver's pale shoulder. "Wanna take a shower?"

"Yeah, that'd be good."

Eugene had already left to go work out before his day of gym clients. Adam could make some coffee, maybe.

"You want fresh clothes to wear home?"

"Mine'll be good enough for BART."

Adam turned on the water and felt it for temperature. He stood up for a kiss, looking into Oliver's grey eyes.

"I'm getting horny again."

"I am too."

"I really have to go to work."

13

IN DOLORES HEIGHTS, Ted operated under the cover of plausible deniability. He opened his laptop on the kitchen table, then poured water for oatmeal into a pan and turned on the burner. Somewhere on his hard drive were Gustavo's papers from when he had taken Ted's class the previous fall. Ted measured the oats. While Gustavo was taking that class, those essays were written for Ted's assignments, but now Ted's position was less clear because he was reading them in his leisure time. They were good papers and worth reading again. Maybe Ted could even make a point of asking Gustavo if it would be okay to quote a passage in class, anonymously, of course. That could be a reason for wanting to examine those artifacts of the term when Ted had been trying to treat Gustavo like every other student in the room. But it didn't matter what shadow-boxing Ted might do. Reading Gustavo's writings now would be a little like watching him unaware.

The water was boiling. Ted closed the file with the essays in it and went to make the oats. He and his colleagues had a meeting later that morning. There would be time for guilty torments when he got home.

.   .   .

On Potrero Hill, Gustavo was a mysterious mountain landscape under the comforter. The top of his hair and a hand stuck out. Jason hadn't even waited to make coffee. Instead, he carefully got his laptop case and brought out the sketchpad and his soft green pencil. He studied the mountain range and drew in some basic contours. Soon Gustavo and the comforter were a series of rounded green shapes. The fingers of the exposed hand were tricky and Jason rendered these clumsily, but managed to capture their geometry. The fingers themselves were beautiful, but Jason could linger over their earthy boyishness later. He was doing one of the timed drawing exercises the book talked about. Just as he was finishing, Gustavo started to move like he might be waking up. Jason quietly put his drawing materials back in the laptop case and headed into the kitchen to start the day.

Richard, well-groomed and confident in a dark red pullover, camel-colored slacks, and loafers, got out of the metro at Montgomery and walked toward the exit. A fashionably pretty young man was completely stopped at the foot of the stairway, standing directly in the middle, doing nothing.

"Excuse me." Richard smiled pleasantly.

After a moment, the stranger looked up, and without a word walked up the steps.

Richard made his way to his usual caffeine outlet for a cup of Darjeeling. At the doorway, he nearly collided with a young woman who cut across his path so she could get to the cream and sugar. He stepped back as quickly as he could to let her pass. She said "sorry" without looking at him or sounding like she meant it.

Carefully weaving through the crowd to his corporate

tower, steaming tea in hand, Richard made it all the way to the elevator bank without spilling. Others were waiting, and he nodded and smiled at them. The doors of one of the elevators opened and he was the last one on. When the doors opened again, Richard stepped out to find someone trying to walk directly into him. Richard just managed to avoid splashing himself with hot tea.

When he arrived at his office, Richard put down the tea, locked his computer to the desk, and headed toward the restroom. Walking toward him in the middle of the corridor was Dustin, the latest hire, directly in his way. Dustin kept on rolling in a straight line. Richard's face registered impatience, then he said, "Excuse me," and swerved out of the way as best he could. Dustin didn't notice that this had happened.

Shortly after, Richard's colleague Mai came out of her office, and he asked her, "Is that the new guy?"

"Yep."

"What a jerk."

"Yep."

At the MFA office, Delma had already settled in for the day when Adam bounced in with flowers for her desk.

"Adam, you silly boy. I didn't know you felt that way about me."

"I'm sharing my love with the world today, Delma!" He booted his computer.

"Hey, go right ahead if it means I get flowers and it's not even my birthday," she said, getting up to find a vase.

"Delma, have you ever stopped to consider that the world is more wonderful because there are redheads in it?"

"I can't say I have, though I suppose it takes all kinds."

"I highly recommend them. They are beautiful and good for the soul."

"You're loopy."

"Loopy with love for humankind."

"Well Ted's gonna need some love when he comes in. He has a big, ugly meeting in a couple of hours."

Upstairs at five minutes to ten, Randall arrived outside Ellen Russo's classroom right as Gustavo showed up. It was the last week of the seminar.

"Hey there, Gustavo."

"Lord Randall! How's it going?"

"It's going well. This seminar has been an amazing experience."

"Truly. I've had so much fun. I'm gonna miss it when it's over."

"I know how you feel. Say, I was wondering if you'd do me a favor and look at something I wrote."

"I'd be glad to. Anytime."

"Thanks. I have it right here."

Randall pulled a folder out of his briefcase and handed it to Gustavo, who carefully put it away in his messenger bag.

"I'll be sure to read this in the next day or two and let you know what I think. By the way, Lacey's is planning another open mic soon. I thought you might be interested in reading again."

"Yes," said Randall, "I'd like that. Thank you for asking. And should you want a ride home, I would be happy to drive you again."

"I wouldn't say no. Jason was really grateful last time. He likes you."

"Gee, I'm pleased to hear that. He's very... delightful."

. . .

At a quarter to one, Ted headed out of the office for a walk. In the lobby, he bumped into Ellen Russo.

"Hey, Ted!" They hugged and she asked him how he was.

"Alive," he said, chuckling, "not terrible. How are you?"

"Doing well, thanks. Almost done here for the summer. Listen, someone in my seminar asked if I knew whatever became of Sal Mariano, and I realized I didn't, which was embarrassing because I felt like I should. And then I almost forgot to follow up on it. Didn't you tell me you knew him slightly?"

"Yeah, I did, though it was a very long time ago."

"Well, if you hear anything about where he is now, let me know, though my student said he'd write Mariano's publisher."

"Interesting. Yeah, if I find out anything, I'll definitely let you know. I think about him from time to time, though I've drifted out of touch with most of the people from that period of my life who are still alive except Peter, my ex. I'll try to ask him next time we talk."

Ellen thanked him, and he went out into the clear, breezy day to make the trek to Lacey's. Gustavo would already be there by the time Ted arrived.

That evening, Adam came home from his workout singing to himself. The gym was so crowded, he was almost crawling over people to get a turn at the equipment, but what did it matter? Everyone was his friend. San Francisco was an enchanted place with beautiful men in it, especially the ones with red-gold hair.

"Must've been a pretty good workout," said Eugene, leaning in the doorway of the kitchen, watching Adam contentedly peel a banana.

"That workout... and the one last night too," Adam grinned, poking the air with the banana, "though I feel like the minute I stop moving, I'm gonna fall asleep standing up."

"Don't worry, I'll get some food together for us in a little bit." Eugene had promised to cook that evening.

Adam went into the living room and made a quick call to Brooklyn. Fred, Adam's father, answered the phone.

"Hey Dad. Is this a good time?"

"Perfect. We just finished dinner and were gonna start a movie: *The Left Handed Gun.* Did you see we won?" Fred was talking about the Mets.

"Yeah, I didn't watch the game but I saw in the paper."

"You being good?"

"Yeah, I robbed a bank and the cops are still looking for me, but I think I can just hole up here till it all blows over."

"Oh yeah—I saw on the news yesterday that you did that," Fred said breezily. "How's Eugene?"

"He's fine."

"How's the job. Is it still okay?"

"Yeah, it's fine. I like the people."

"It's always the people. Let me get your mother." Fred held the receiver away from his face. "Marleen, it's Adam."

Adam's mother took the phone. "Hiya sweetheart. How's San Francisco?"

"More wonderful than you can imagine, Ma."

"Are you okay?"

"Yeah, I'm fine."

"Good. Is Eugene okay?"

"Yeah, he's fine. He's in the kitchen making dinner."

"Please tell him how much I love him."

Eugene's phone rang while he was cooking. He normally didn't answer if he was working in the kitchen, but he gave in and looked. It was Cody.

"Hey Cody, nice to hear from you!"

"Hey there, Eugene." His voice sounded sexy. "How are you today?"

"Just making some dinner here."

"What are you making?"

"Chicken-tofu stir fry and couscous."

"That sounds good."

"You wanna come over? It's just me and Adam here, but I made enough for three."

"Thanks, but I can't right now. I just wanted to say hello and see how you were."

After he finished up with Cody, Eugene found Adam and told him to come eat.

"My mother said to say how much she loves you."

"Everything okay?"

"Yeah, they're fine," said Adam, taking two beers from the fridge.

"Cody just called."

"How's he doing?"

"There's something about that guy that I somehow just don't get."

The doorbell rang. It was Randall.

"Greetings. I hope I'm not interrupting."

Adam let him in, explaining that they were about to eat.

"There's enough for three if you wanna stay," Eugene said.

"Thanks. I wouldn't want to impose."

"Nah, come sit down," said Adam, grabbing utensils from a drawer. "You want a beer?"

"Thanks, I'd love one. I was in the neighborhood and thought I'd stop by to see if you guys wanted to go to Punk Night later this week. My friend Marty's band Swapped Condoms is playing."

"Oh man, gross name!" Eugene groaned while trying to plate some food for Randall.

"They're a punk band. Would you have expected something tasteful?"

"Even so... ugh!"

Looking pleased with himself for being disgusting, Randall asked, "Are you gentlemen going to the fair on Sunday?" Adam and Eugene didn't know what he meant. "You're kidding. You really don't know about this? It's a huge celebration of kink. Every perv within driving distance will be there getting his freak on. People even fly in for this event."

"Hey, wait a minute," said Eugene with sudden recognition, "one of my clients at the gym was talking about this."

"Oh yeah," said Adam, "now that I think about it, I've seen ads for it, but I didn't know what it was supposed to be about."

"I knew you guys had to have at least heard of this event. You should go. Your visit to San Francisco wouldn't be complete without it."

14

THURSDAY EVENING, South of Market. The show hadn't started yet when Randall arrived with Duane, Adam, and Eugene. They got earplugs from a gumball machine to reduce the noise, sat down at the bar, and ordered drinks. Swapped Condoms was setting up. Duane looked around the room and noticed that Seth was there too, sitting by himself.

"Marty's the one with the long, black hair," said Randall. "He plays bass. If I catch his eye, I'll introduce you."

Catching Marty's eye might have taken some work since he was wearing aviator sunglasses. The rest of the outfit consisted of a tight black t-shirt with the sleeves cut off, tight black pants and engineer boots almost bigger than the rest of him. He was about five-foot-six and 120 pounds.

"Hey, would you excuse me a moment?" said Duane. "Sorry, I don't mean to be rude but I see someone I know over there and just wanna say hi."

"Please, go right ahead," said Randall. He turned to Adam and Eugene. "Have you guys been here before?"

"We haven't," said Adam, looking around the wildly decorated biker bar. "Very cool."

At that moment, Marty came to the bar for beers for the band.

"Hey Marty!" Randall waved.

"Oh hey," said Marty in a voice like wet paper. "Thanks for coming out to see us tonight."

"I know you're busy, so I won't keep you, but these are my friends Adam and Eugene."

"Hey," said Marty, who picked up the beers and walked away.

"Duane! Oh my gawd, what are you doing here?" Seth said in a tired voice, going in for a hug. "I got your message. I'm sorry I didn't call. I've just felt so fucked up. I wouldn't even be out tonight, but I just had to get out of the house for a while or I'd go crazy."

"Gosh, I'm sorry to hear you're having a bad time," said Duane. "You look good, anyway."

"Thanks. I don't feel pretty right now. I've been really stressed out lately. And this is sort of TMI but I have a zit on my ass."

Duane guffawed and then immediately apologized. "Sorry, I don't mean to laugh. A zit on the ass is really miserable."

"It fucking hurts and I have to sit leaning to one side and I just don't feel pretty. As if I didn't have enough to deal with already. I have a friend in the second band, Skinny Snotty Fairy, but I don't know if I'll stay. I told him I'd see."

"Well, at least no one here can see the zit on your ass, and you're as handsome as ever."

"Thank you. You're a kind friend."

"Heck, I bet I wouldn't even care about the zit if you wanted to come to my place a little later."

"Thanks—normally, that would sound really good but I just don't know. I can barely even stand myself right now. Anyway, I didn't mean to go on about that. What are you up to tonight? Did you come for the show?"

"Yeah. I'm with those guys over there. The really tall one's my work buddy. He knows a dude in Swapped Condoms."

"Vile band name but the one with the bleached hair is hot," Seth said, watching them move equipment around the stage. "Anyway, I don't want to take you away from your friends. I should probably be home anyway."

"Well if you change your mind and want to hang out, let me know."

"Thanks. My ass really hurts."

When Duane rejoined the others, Randall had gone to the bathroom. Adam and Eugene asked Duane if everything was okay since Seth looked unhappy.

"He's having a rough night."

"You missed meeting Marty," said Eugene.

"Yeah," said Adam. "Sort of."

"That was pretty underwhelming," Eugene agreed. "Five bucks says these guys stink."

It was clear by the end of the first song that Swapped Condoms wasn't very good. During a short break, Adam pulled out an earplug to hear Eugene say, "Sounds like every other crappy punk band."

"At least the dude with the messed-up hair is very porkable," Adam noted.

The set ended. Even Randall seemed to agree that the front man with the popcorn-colored hair and dark roots was the most entertaining part of the experience though not necessarily for musical reasons. Adam and Eugene avoided giving their opinion of Marty.

. . .

It was Sunday morning and Gustavo wasn't going to the fair. He had traded with a friend at Lacey's and agreed to be in the store that day. Jason was going with Mike, James, and Troy, who had all decided to wear matching harnesses and short shorts. Gustavo watched admiringly as Jason stood in front of the mirror on the back of the bedroom door, studying himself in his kinky outfit, looking irresistibly cute and cuddly. The hint of butteriness all over him gave an impression of a Renaissance cherub and found its ultimate glory in his high, round, plump little bottom. He frowned.

"Do I look okay?"

Gustavo told him, "I could eat you with a spoon."

"Hm..." said Jason skeptically.

"You should be wearing those little pants when I come home, if some other guy hasn't carried you off over his shoulder first. If I didn't have to go to work, you'd never make it to the fair."

The weather was mild and not too windy. South of Market, tons of people were decked out in their fetish finery. Adam and Eugene had met Oliver at the Civic Center BART station and walked down together. When Adam had invited Oliver, he said he didn't know if it would be Oliver's idea of fun, and mentioned that Randall would be there as well. But Oliver had replied that he wanted to go. Now the two of them and Eugene were waiting inside the fair at 9th and Folsom for Randall to show up... with Marty.

"Marty the Swapped Condom." Adam was grinning.

Eugene groaned.

"You guys really don't like him," said Oliver.

Adam suggested that the reason might be obvious when Marty arrived. But when Randall showed up, he was alone and apologetic.

"Marty couldn't make it. He said he had to visit his family."

The idea of Marty having a family seemed improbable, but it obviously wasn't impossible.

Adam said nonchalantly, "Too bad Marty couldn't make it," but there was still a little lingering awkwardness.

"Well," said Randall, "I guess we'll just soldier on. Would anyone like to accompany me to the beer booth over there and purchase what will probably be an insipid, watery beverage?"

Drinking the unremarkable beer, Duane wandered the fair alone. For a while, he watched a flogging demonstration, then checked out the kinky gear for sale in the booths. Some guys got freaky right in the street, which created a lot of excitement. Spectators took photos of the action but Duane just watched for a few seconds and moved on. The fun of the fair was in the moment. There were hundreds of faces, outfits, and bodies to bug out on. The muscle boys were almost a distinct species in their armbands and magazine-like faces. There were the regulation sunbaked nudists. Old men in bespoke leather uniforms wore pins and patches like World War II veterans, which some of them may have been, for all Duane knew. There was the usual crowd of townies out for yet another street fair. And there were the baby animals playing in the sunshine: the young guys at the fair for the first time.

Jason and Mike and James and Troy in their matching outfits lapped at the bad drinks, ate hot dogs, browsed the booths, goggled at some guys having sex in the street, dared each other to get whipped but didn't, sighed for studs they didn't know they could get, were cruised by bulls they walked right by without seeing, and had a blast. Drawn in by the hunks at the booth of a porn company, they were each handed a business card and told they should make a movie, which made them giggle and wonder for a moment if they really would.

Steve and Hector were having fun flirting with the boys who drifted by their tent. Steve was feeling a little more in tune with the whole event that year. The two models who had come by to help out for a while were good company. Hector was looking cubbishly sexy in a bar vest and fatigues that showed off his assets. And suddenly, Steve saw Eugene walking in their direction.

"Hey Hector, look who's here!"

"Eugene!" said Hector, stepping to the front of the booth. "What's going on? Are you here by yourself?"

"I'm with friends. They're checking out the flogging."

"No flogging for you?" asked Steve.

"I think I'll pass for now."

Steve introduced Eugene to the two models, Paolo and Micah, who were similar to Eugene in age and build, and were watching him with interest. The boys talked for a little while, and it was all very cruise-y. Finally, Eugene needed to check in with his friends.

"We're going to a party later," said Micah. "Maybe you'd like to come."

Duane wandered over to the doorway of a crowded bar and showed his ID, but there was a long wait inside at the well. Eventually, he got a cup of cheap beer and tried to find a place to stand. The room was very full. He got as comfortable as he could and drank his beer in the crush of bodies. Some dude wanted to make out, so Duane smiled and made out. After a while, he said to his new friend, "I wanna dance." And he put the beer cup down somewhere and headed out into the light without looking to see if anyone followed him.

Eugene had caught up with the others. "How was the flogging?"

"Pretty intense, I'd have to say," said Randall appreciatively. Randall knew his flogging. "And the guy getting flogged was really cute."

"I dunno," joked Adam, "seems like I see one flog, I've seen 'em all."

Randall spotted Duane leaving the bar. "Say, there goes Duane." Randall headed toward him and the others followed. "Hey Duane!"

Duane looked around and brightened when he saw Randall. He waved and came strolling over. "Well, hello there. Nice to see you. Hey, you guys," he said, seeing Adam and Eugene. They introduced him to Oliver. "Does anyone wanna dance?"

Randall said he could go for some dancing, as he was hoping vaguely that it might get him some action. Adam was hungry and wanted a sausage. Eugene excused himself, saying he wanted to talk to Steve and Hector about something.

After the others had gone, Adam said to Oliver, "Are you hungry? I'm thinking about a Polish sausage. But you probably don't eat street fair food."

"I could eat a veggie burger."

"Arright—let's find you a veggie burger."

On the quest for food, Oliver said, "I get why Eugene's your best friend. He's a good guy."

"Yes, Eugene is a good guy."

They found a concession stand with veggie and non-veggie burgers, and took away one of each to eat as best they could standing up.

Swallowing a mouthful and trying not to make too big a pig of himself, Adam asked, "And what did you think of the flogging, Mr. Oliver?"

"It was, um, sort of exciting." He was smiling shyly.

Adam couldn't believe it.

"What? You'd like that?"

"Well, maybe not right in the middle of my back."

Adam laughed, completely stunned.

"Aw, man—I don't think I could do that to someone! You'd want me to hit you like that? And your skin is so beautiful! I couldn't do that to you. Do you really want that? Are you laughing at me? Why are you laughing?"

On the dance floor, Jason and Mike and James and Troy had found some humpy older boys who were only too happy to bust a move with them. Jason noticed Duane dancing with another guy Jason knew, a friend of Gustavo's who was at the store one night and gave them a ride. They weren't all that nearby and didn't see him. Jason smiled to himself.

Adam and Oliver made out against the side of a building. Right in the street. Then they noticed how much attention they were getting and decided to go to Adam's place for a while.

The fog started coming in, and the wind picked up. Jason and Mike and James and Troy were all tuckered out after all the fun, and giggled and hugged and made their way home.

Randall scored a hot, freaky leather dude.

Eugene went to check out a couple of parties.

And Duane just kept on dancing.

In a house somewhere in the tangle of streets that was Eureka Valley, the Lavender Engineers were enjoying a spectacular view of the city and some wonderfully tender steak skewers with chimichurri made by Chuck. Richard poured Cabernet Sauvignon from their new decanter. ("Napa?" "Paso Robles.")

Aaron was considering trading in the SUV for something smaller because gas was so expensive, but on the other hand, it sure was nice for camping in the desert with the telescope. Kyle complained about driving down to Mountain View every day. He thought about taking the train, but the service was hit or miss, and besides, he'd have to spend all that time in transit. Jeff suggested he could drive down to 22nd Street and take the train from there. He might get a lot of work done sitting on the train. Richard was lucky to work downtown and could leave his car at home most of the time. That was obviously the right thing to do. Jeff wondered if self-driving vehicles would ever really be a thing. Maybe there could be a shuttle to Mountain View, Chuck suggested. Like a private bus company or something. Richard wondered if this was such a good idea. But then he worked in the same city in which he lived.

Mark's mother was coming to town, and of course he and Kyle were looking forward to seeing her, though they wished they had a bigger house. Aaron and Jeff, who did have a bigger house, said that a Mom visit cramped their style no matter what. Not that they didn't enjoy her company too, but they had to be with her the whole time. Chuck wondered if they could just offer to put her up in a hotel, but maybe she would feel like they didn't really want her around. In Jeff's case, it was true but they couldn't let her think that. Besides, there was a shortage of hotel rooms in the city. Chuck joked that wouldn't it be great if you could just stick her in someone else's guest bedroom instead. Or a vacant apartment. There could be a whole industry based on stashing out-of-town guests in other people's apartments. Everyone laughed and thought it was a great idea.

Richard showed off the new lens he had purchased at Hengist Photography. Kyle said he had heard that they were closing after fifty-five years in business. Mark thought it was a shame, and everyone agreed. Chuck said Richard should take a picture of everyone there, but no one wanted his picture taken. Richard said that was fine and snapped a few shots of the buildings downtown. Jeff and Aaron made appreciative comments about the new lens before mentioning the new telescope they were buying. Richard said he very much wanted to see the telescope when it arrived. They really were going to go on that camping trip.

15

RANDALL SHOWED up for lunch with Adam at a café near CUE wearing interview clothes. He had just met with the manager of a photo equipment rental place in the East Bay.

"Man, I feel for you," said Adam. "I'm gonna be looking myself soon, and it is very crappy."

"I dunno, I'm trying to think of it as an adventure. Conrad was really nice and told us we would get paid for any time we spent interviewing. Anyway, it'll keep me out of trouble for a while now that the seminar's over."

"You haven't said anything lately about the Sal Mariano search. Did you ever find out more?"

"No. I wrote to the publisher but haven't heard back. And I just couldn't see myself ringing the doorbell."

"The publisher might still write you back. It could take a while."

"Yeah, it might," Randall said, none too assertively. "Anyway, this job search is a big change. I should focus on getting my life together a little. I'm thinking about getting into shape by taking up yoga."

"Doesn't surfing keep you pretty fit?"

"Yeah, it does in some ways, but I'm not all that elastic. Melissa at work suggested I should improve my alignment, which I take to mean I have the posture of a knuckle-dragger. I'm also thinking I could study tantric sex and learn to be able to do things only a dog can do."

"That sounds cool. You could go fuck yourself."

"Exactly. But I'm kind of afraid of those pissy little yoga studios."

"You could try my gym. They have yoga classes. A bunch of the people who work out there are stuck-up assholes but you see all types. The classes look like they might be okay."

Randall said he'd check it out.

"And you should talk to Eugene since he'll know the instructors. He could probably tell you more about it than I can."

"This is going to make me look like a Greek god," said Steve between sets, breathing hard.

"That's a hard goal to quantify," said Eugene.

"I try to leave room for interpretation."

"Can you see the changes yet?"

"Maybe? I think so, but I wonder if it's just wishful thinking. Hector says he sees a difference."

"That's always a good sign when someone else notices."

"Of course, I really want to believe him. Anyway, we went hiking earlier this week, and I swear I could feel the difference."

"Even better," said Eugene. "So you guys went hiking," he added distractedly. "I'll bet Hector looks good breaking a sweat."

"Oh yeah?" Steve smiled. "I think the two of you might have fun together. Hector's more than a little interested."

Eugene said he had suspected as much, starting from the day he tried on the superhero costume for them.

"Hector just bought a superhero suit of his own for cosplay, and I gotta say he looks insanely hot in it. One of the models, a skinny little kid, turns out to be crazy for big, well-padded guys and is hoping Superbear will rescue him. We're thinking of making a movie around it."

"Well, maybe you wouldn't mind if I borrow Superbear some night, if he's available."

"I wouldn't mind one bit. There's plenty to share. And I believe you young guys should get all the fun you can."

Adam and Oliver planned to meet South of Market for dinner after work. Oliver wasn't all that good with restaurants in San Francisco but he had been to a Thai place he liked well enough.

"I think that's near a high-quality fetish store Randall told me about," said Adam. "Do you wanna check it out?" He was starting to sound less shocked that Oliver could like those kinds of things.

"I wouldn't mind, but we don't need to do that together if you don't want to."

"Well, it could be interesting. Who knows? Maybe I'll see something I didn't even know I'd like."

It didn't take long for them to decide dinner could wait. The shop was only a few blocks from the restaurant. When they got there, it was big and full of all sorts of things they hadn't seen before, even in porn. ("Wow, I wouldn't have thought that was possible.") Obviously clueless about what they were doing, they got a lot of friendly attention from the staff. The other shoppers noticed them too. Adam was a little shy, but game and definitely intrigued. Oliver was even more shy but too excited to let that stop him from getting into it. They were intrigued by the play clothes, puzzling over buckles, straps, and shiny metal rings.

Adam pointed out some wrestling singlets. "I wrestled in

high school but maybe these are for a different kind of wrestling."

"You'd look good in one," Oliver said.

"Maybe."

They browsed the paddles and floggers, and Oliver was definitely curious, but he needed to think about what he'd want. It was too much new information.

As they left to go eat, Adam asked Oliver if any of the leather or rubber outfits turned him on. Oliver didn't really understand what most of it was supposed to be about but thought the singlets might be fun.

"I'd like to see you in one of the ones with the open ass," said Adam, starting to get into what gear he might like to try out with Oliver.

"I'd wear one of those for you."

"You would, Mr. Oliver?"

Oliver nodded and smiled.

"But you know what really gets me crazy?" said Adam. "Plain, nerdy, white cotton briefs with the fly."

"Yeah, those are sexy."

"Hottest underwear ever."

In the early morning grey on Market Street, Randall arrived on time if a little foggy for Yoga with Liam. He parked the van, grabbed his bag and yoga mat from the back seat and stumbled through the door of the gym. At ten minutes to seven, the place was busy. Randall headed for the locker room, dodging a typical range of self-absorbed gym bods, to change into a pair of shorts. Turning a corner, he almost collided with a lanky hippie with a light brown beard and dreadlocks. This was jarring until the hippie smiled vapidly and said, "I'm sorry, brother. Have a good workout!" The hippie was extremely hot.

Liam, the class instructor, turned out to be a dance bully,

but Randall applied himself as best he could and soon was doing yoga, approximately. His efforts were undermined when he noticed the hippie from the locker room was a couple of yoga mats forward and to the right, giving a mostly unobstructed view of his rear end. Dreadlocks weren't really Randall's thing, but in this case, he had interesting little filigree rings in them. He also had sexy, flared nostrils and shapely feet. When Yoga with Liam was over, Randall made a point of not staring while they were getting dressed, though he managed to say in a calm voice, "That was a great class."

"Wasn't it? I signed up for it just so I could work with this instructor. He's amazing!"

What was so amazing about Liam might have been lost on someone like Randall, who just said he was a beginner and found it a little hard to follow what was going on. The dreadlocked stranger, whose name was Drew, had studied yoga for a while but was learning so much from this beginner class because of Liam.

"You sound like you really know what you're doing," said Randall. "I only blundered into this because a friend of mine told me I need to pay closer attention to alignment."

"Alignment is so important," said Drew, his eyes widening.

"Say, maybe you'd be willing to give me some pointers about that. Would you like to get coffee or something to eat?"

"That would be great! Recovery after exercise is so important."

Recovery took the form of eggs, potatoes, and toast. Over breakfast, Randall learned Drew had recently arrived from Long Beach. At the moment, he was staying in the Mission with some friends who had started a personal care and supplement company called Earthy Luvin'. Drew thought their products were really great and hoped to help market them, though he didn't know yet how that would happen. Right now, he worked in a plant store. Drew liked San Francisco but was thinking of moving to Santa Cruz.

"Santa Cruz is one of my favorite places," said Randall. "The surfing is great there."

"I love surfing! Maybe you could show me where the good spots are up here, if that wouldn't be giving any secrets away."

"I'd be happy to show you the place where I surf at Ocean Beach," said Randall. "Listen, I'm wondering about something and maybe I could ask you. Do you know anything about tantric yoga?"

"Now that's a very interesting subject," Drew said, sounding serious, "but some traditions place too great an emphasis on semen retention, a practice I believe to be unnecessary and dangerous to prostate health."

"I'm no expert," said Randall, "but it seems like we're meant to orgasm as much as possible."

Drew couldn't have agreed more.

"I have forty-five minutes before I need to get ready for work," said Randall. "Would you like to see where I surf?"

"That would be amazing!"

Later that day, Gustavo was working at Lacey's when Orion walked in with his usual air of manly confidence.

"Hey Orion. How's it going?"

"Terrific. I saw the poster in the window for the next open mic. Are you planning to read something?"

"Yeah, probably so, but you should come regardless. It'll be a great evening."

"I'll be there. Hey, I'm having a party at Molly's on Thursday to promote a young musician friend of mine. Have I told you about Marty? He's staying with me for a few weeks while he looks for a longer-term living arrangement. I really think you'll like him. He's in a great punk band."

Gustavo said he would try to make it, and Orion went on his way.

A little later, Ted Schacter came in. Gustavo greeted him with a big smile.

"You keeping busy now that the seminar is over?" Ted asked.

"Yeah, I already miss it, but I'm also happy to have time to breathe and pay more attention to the everyday stuff."

They talked about what classes Gustavo should take in the fall. Gustavo asked about the MFA program and if Ted thought he should apply. Ted hoped he would. They laughed and made jokes in the usual way. At no point did Ted say anything about how the central administration told him and his colleagues that morning that, to their great disappointment, a merger with Yerba Buena University wouldn't be possible. The other school was having trouble resolving some problems of its own—not enough to sink it, but it was too weak to acquire CUE. The possibility Ted and his colleagues least wanted to entertain was a real one: they might need to graduate their last class. Ted had broken the news to Delma in confidence. He had no reason yet to tell Adam.

Ted browsed in Lacey's for a while, bought a book, and wished Gustavo a good evening. His next stop was the taqueria before trudging up 20th Street toward home. Once inside the door, he dropped his briefcase, put the burrito in the kitchen and took off his work drag. He had eaten half the burrito when the phone rang. It was Peter, his ex.

"Hey love. I'm glad you called."

"What's wrong? You sound upset."

"Not my best day. CUE might not be able to turn things around."

"Crap."

"Yeah, I know. We're going to talk to California Collegiate.

They were on the list of possibilities before but we're already short on resources—time, especially. I dunno. We'll see."

California Collegiate University was made up of a group of essentially autonomous constituent colleges with a central administration. At that moment, they hadn't approached California Collegiate, so they were an unknown quantity. Even if they were to step in, Ted worried about whether that might change the character of CUE too much, maybe even lose some programs, though the more pressing concern was whether there would be anything at all to rescue.

"How are things otherwise? Is your mom okay?" Peter asked.

"She's stable at the moment. Dave and I think she can be independent for a while longer but it's good he's close."

"Would you ever move back East?"

"Not sure. At the moment, I'm considering all options. For instance, I could go live in a cave."

"Yeah, you could, but wherever you are, I don't think you'll have trouble finding a teaching job."

"That might be true, though I'd just like to know if I should be applying for one tomorrow. Right now, I can't think straight long enough to focus on anything, and it's burning me out."

"I'm sorry, hon—I feel terrible for you."

"Well, the misery can't go on forever. And the situation isn't completely hopeless. We still don't know what's gonna happen. But let's talk about something else. Do you wanna have dinner this weekend?"

"Yeah, sure. Saturday would be good."

"Okay, good. And there was something else I was supposed to ask you about. I can't think what it was."

16

Early Sunday afternoon, Adam got out of the train in downtown Berkeley. It was his first trip to the other side of the Bay. Oliver was waiting for him, looking very handsome and somehow more relaxed on his own turf. He led the way to a nearby brewpub where they ordered some lunch and a couple of beers.

"It feels very different over here," said Adam. They were sitting with their pints, waiting for their food to arrive. "I dunno, maybe it's because it's a university town. But I like it."

When they finished eating, they walked along Shattuck, then turned east on Center Street. Suddenly, they were in a small wooded area in the middle of everything. Oliver pointed to some ivy and explained they were walking through a part of the campus where the local community was trying to remove invasive species of plants and reintroduce native ones.

"It's like we stepped off the street into a forest," said Adam.

"That stream over there is Strawberry Creek. It starts as two creeks in the hills, and they converge at this point here on campus. Then it goes into that culvert over there and runs underneath the streets of Berkeley."

In the cool green shade, Oliver's skin seemed particularly translucent. He was also very delectable. Adam said, "C'mere a minute." He held Oliver in his arms and kissed him.

They followed the stream across a couple of bridges, coming out of the trees near an indoor basketball arena. There they saw two punk boys standing by the wall. When the other dudes noticed Adam and Oliver looking, they grinned.

Adam said to Oliver, "I'm picking up a signal on the long-range gaydar, Captain."

He winked at the punks and one of them called out, "Hey guy!"

As Adam and Oliver walked east toward Bancroft, the two punks flirted with them for a while until they passed out of sight.

"They were hot," Adam said. "Funny, too."

Oliver sighed. "That never happens to me when I'm by myself."

He showed Adam an eccentrically shaped concrete building that housed the Art Museum, and they decided to check it out. The inside was made up of cantilevered platforms that hung out into open space. At that moment it was practically deserted, which added to its sci-fi strangeness.

"This is really cool," said Adam.

"Yeah, it's too bad they don't get more visitors."

Adam hugged Oliver from behind, nuzzling his neck. "But I might boff you right here and no one would know."

Oliver laughed. "That's a funny word."

"I think it's beautiful," said Adam, still holding Oliver close with his left hand and raising the other hand in front of them both in an oratory gesture. "'Boff... *boff*....' Or I could've said that I might *boink* you right here. That's good too."

"I like 'boff.'"

"Excellent, my good fellow. Then I will boff you anytime you desire."

When they were back outside, Oliver led them along the rows of Greek houses and other student residences, past People's Park and down Telegraph Avenue. They browsed in Moe's Books for a while, then found a café and had something to drink. They couldn't believe it when they saw it was already close to six o'clock.

"When do you have to be home?" Adam asked.

Oliver had told his family he would eat with them that evening. "I should leave pretty soon. Maybe I should call them in case I'm a little late."

Adam tactfully stood a little way off while Oliver dialed the number. After a brief conversation, Oliver came closer to Adam but was still on the call.

"My mom is asking if you'd like to come over for dinner."

Adam said, "Sure, I'd be glad to."

As they walked to the BART station, Adam smiled like it was totally normal to be going home with Oliver to meet his family for the first time and have dinner at their table. They went into the station and caught a train to MacArthur, then caught another. And they got out at Rockridge and walked past pleasant, comfortable-looking houses with basketball hoops and planters and flowers, and nice kids playing out front, and cats on the porch, and dogs being walked by friendly looking people. And they stopped in front of one of the houses.

Oliver looked at Adam. "Ready?"

They went in through the back into a craftsman kitchen with an aroma of something savory in the oven. Beneath that was a warm background smell of dried fruit and baking spices. Adam caught a glimpse of a bright, airy dining room off to one side. A small woman with ginger curls and smile lines around her twinkling blue eyes came toward them from the sink.

"Hi Adam, I'm Jeannette. Nice to meet you." She dried her right hand on a towel, then put it out to Adam to shake as she offered the boys a glass of white wine.

Adam and Oliver sat in the living room with their wine while Jeannette moved around the house, drifting in and out, talking to them as she passed by, a moving field of energy. Adam looked around at the books in the bookcases next to the tiled fireplace, and at the paintings and photos on the walls.

"I hope this is okay," said Oliver, a little sheepishly.

"It's totally okay. I really like your mom."

"Everybody does."

Jeannette was as voluble as Oliver was quiet, chatting in an offhand way to the boys, to herself, and to a small, slate-grey cat named Zephyr who rubbed her face against Adam's sneakers. In a while, Oliver's dad came downstairs, and it was obvious which parent Oliver took after, though Oliver was more intense. Erik, on the other hand, seemed to be thinking of something far away. He was blond and a little taller than his son, and had a gentle smile. He greeted Oliver and the visitor, spoke with Jeannette for a moment, then went back upstairs.

Shortly after Erik left the room, Lilly, a red-headed girl of twenty, bounced through the front door, said hello, introduced herself, and went upstairs to take a shower.

Jeannette came in with a glass of wine for herself, sat down, and pushed a coppery lock behind an ear. "We're having eggplant parmigiana and baked chicken. I thought I heard Lilly come in."

The boys told her she had.

"She's been hiking in Tilden with her friends. I wouldn't have minded something like that myself today, but I had too much to do around the house. I love the eggplant but it takes a while to make. Thanks for coming over to meet us, Adam. I think Oliver told me you're visiting from Brooklyn?"

"That's right. I'm here for the summer."

"It must be very different here."

"It is. I'm not missing the muggy weather."

"Yeah, I'd imagine New York in August must get pretty uncomfortable," said Jeannette, making a face.

"Yeah, it does." Adam took a deep breath and exhaled. "I guess it's already the first week of August."

The sheer curtains over the windows diffused green light from the front garden. Jeannette talked with Adam about Manhattan and downtown Brooklyn, both of which she had seen, and about how San Francisco was less densely urban than New York though more so than Oakland. She asked Adam if he was old enough to remember Times Square before they cleaned it up, and he said that he was. Then Erik came downstairs to help with dinner, and he and Jeannette disappeared into the kitchen.

When the boys were alone, Adam asked, "Do your folks know we're, um...?"

"Yeah, I think so."

It had been some time since Adam had eaten with his own family or anyone else's. Jeannette laid out an impressive spread, jumping up to bring out vegetables while they were still hot. Lilly told everyone about her adventure in Tilden Park, and the boys talked about their day in Berkeley. Adam answered questions about New York again.

Adam noticed Lilly looking at him with amused skepticism. After a while, she said to him, eyes narrowed, "Hm... you *like* my brother."

Later, in the living room when the boys had a moment to themselves, Oliver said, "They like you."

"It's mutual." After a moment, Adam asked when he should get on BART. Oliver excused himself and went to the kitchen.

When he came back, he said shyly, "It would be okay if you stayed over."

"Man, I feel like I'm blushing." Adam blinked hard and thought for a moment. "It would be a pretty rough start in the morning, wouldn't it? I'd have to go home early enough to get dressed for work."

"I'd go to the station with you."

To Adam's relief, Oliver's childhood bedroom had a full-sized bed. Jeannette had put a towel and a toothbrush in the bathroom for him, which was somehow embarrassing and nice at the same time.

"You're more of a brainiac than me," said Adam, looking around Oliver's room at the books and school awards. "I'll bet you're smarter too."

Oliver shrugged dismissively. "I dunno about that."

Adam put his hands around Oliver's hips. The boys kissed and Adam felt under Oliver's shirt, up his back and down into his waistband.

"Tighty-whities?"

Oliver nodded, and Adam held him close.

In the early morning, Adam went off without too much grumbling about his painful commute. They had a last hug outside of the fare gate and a little wave when Adam was on the other side. And then he was on his own in a crowded train of strangers on their way to San Francisco.

17

TANTRA, it turned out, was not exactly what Randall had imagined, but something far more rewarding—a means of balancing the body and quieting the mind. It offered a path for meeting the chaos of the world with detachment. A new and energizing discipline was open to him if he invested a little time in it. He began each morning practicing a sequence of the asanas he had learned in class, then greeted the day with calm focus. The essential thing to remember was to let go of whatever was beyond his control.

One morning, Randall was a little later than usual leaving the apartment, but incorporating a new routine would take time. Instead of waiting for the streetcar to take him to Montgomery Street, he drove. He ran the risk of having trouble finding parking or having to pay for a garage for the day, but this small experiment was a drop in the ocean.

At a red light, another car was to his right. Its windows were dark and the bass was booming. He assumed the other driver would try to zip out in front. So with an out-breath, Randall calmly let the car in front of him when the light changed to green. It was easy to do. In the vast, ever-changing kaleidoscope of the universe, a few minutes that day would make no difference. There was no need to hurry.

Finding a place to park South of Market shortly before ten o'clock in the morning was always challenging but something was sure to open up. Randall was serene and didn't rush. It was a matter of leaving room for the event to happen. As he turned onto 2nd Street, another vehicle changed lanes without signaling, cutting him off, then slowed down. Randall leaned on his horn, then suddenly relaxed, took an in-breath, and let it go. No reason to get upset. Just at that moment, he saw a parking spot. Suddenly, a driver much farther ahead without any lights flashing backed up a quarter of a block to take it. Randall yelled out the passenger-side window, "Fuck you, jackass! Why don't you go shit in your hat?!" He tried breathing slowly and rhythmically. A new mindset was going to take time.

After about fifteen minutes, Randall finally found parking a few long South of Market blocks away and strolled toward Hengist. As he was walking along, some hipster talking on his phone insisted on heading directly toward Randall, who was trying to keep to the right. Randall tried to pass and the other guy mirrored him.

"Jesus Christ on a bike, asswipe! Are you fucking high?!"

When Randall stomped into the store, he apologized to Duane. "Sorry I'm late—I started taking yoga."

Randall went to the staff area upstairs, put his jacket and briefcase away and signed in. When he returned to the salesroom, Duane let him know the store hadn't been all that busy and asked how he was liking yoga.

"Actually, it's pretty cool. I met this wild faerie type," Randall laughed. "He's way out there but he's an amazing lay."

"That's always good," said Duane. "Hey, tell me again when the open mic is? I thought I'd try to make it this time, if that's okay."

"Please do. It's Wednesday of next week."

"Do you have something written for it?"

"Yeah, I think so, but I might try to do a new one over the weekend. I just had an interesting idea for a piece that's all about how the city is filling up with douchebags."

At lunch, Duane called Seth to see if he'd like to go out Thursday. Seth said he was going to a party but maybe Duane would like to come along.

"There's this guy I know—Orion. This thing's supposed to be for his latest boytoy or whatever. He's in some punk band. I dunno—maybe it'll be fun. It's at Molly's, at the bottom of Potrero Hill."

It was early evening. Adam was racing down the sidewalk to get to Dolores Park in order not to be late. He was supposed to meet Oliver by the tennis courts. Oliver had his bike with him and had gotten there with no trouble at all. The weather was very pleasant, perfect for hanging out by the tennis courts, watching the world go by while waiting for someone. Too perfect to spend hurrying down the street, paying no attention to how beautiful everything was at that moment.

Finally, Adam arrived sweaty and out of breath, only a couple of minutes late.

"Sorry I'm late," he said, panting slightly.

"You're not that late. I didn't mind waiting."

"Well, that's good, at least. So what would you like for dinner?"

"Not sure," said Oliver.

"We could go for Thai."

"We could," Oliver agreed, then added, "It's so nice out."

"Yes, it is," said Adam. "I guess if you're not too hungry, maybe we could find a place to sit for a while and think about where to go?"

"Okay, sure."

Oliver locked up his bike and they strolled around the park. The tennis and basketball courts were all busy as they passed by. Across the street, a few students lingered in front of Mission High. People were out having a good time.

"How was your day?" asked Oliver.

"About like usual." said Adam.

"Same here."

They got to the corner by the J Church tracks and walked along the high western edge of the park. In the distance, kids were screaming and running around. It was the sort of evening that brought the whole city to life, but both boys were quiet. Finally, Adam said, "I liked meeting your family."

"They really liked you. Sorry if it was weird asking you to come home with me."

"I could've said no. I really did want to meet them." Adam watched some dogs playing for a while. There was a little one who wanted to be chased, and the other dogs all followed it around the grass.

Suddenly Adam said, "Can I ask you a hypothetical question about something that's been on my mind?"

"Yeah, sure. Go ahead."

"If you had a boyfriend, would it matter to you whether or not he was very ambitious?"

Oliver smiled. "Not really, though I'd hope he was doing some kind of work that made him happy."

Adam frowned.

"That's my problem right there. I have no idea what I'm supposed to be doing. I feel like in order for it to be fulfilling, it would need to be an actual career of some kind."

"Maybe not every career is ambitious. Maybe it could be something simple."

"I feel like if it were so simple, I'd know what it was. But I don't. Right now, all I know is that I don't want to end up in some random job and say, 'Oh well, I guess it's a living.' I feel like I'm supposed to have a plan or else I could be doing that dumb job until I got a different one. And then I'd be stuck doing that for a while until something else came along."

They walked in silence for a minute or two, then chose a bench on the south side of the park, which gave a view of downtown in the distance. A bunch of forty-year-olds had brought a picnic and were playing games on the grass while a black Lab chewed a tennis ball between its front paws. An elderly couple carefully made their way down the slope past the playground.

Oliver said, "Can *I* ask *you* something hypothetically?"

"Yes, of course."

"Do you think monogamy matters at all?"

Adam was surprised by the question but not for long.

"I dunno. I guess so? It would depend on the two people."

"Yeah, probably, huh?" Oliver sounded pensive and unsettled.

"Well," Adam asked, looking out at the view, "do you believe people can be happy in an open relationship?"

"That might depend on the situation too. The idea seems okay in theory, but for some reason, it still makes me nervous."

"You mean because someone could bring home something you don't want to catch?"

"Well, yeah, there's that. I let myself get freaked out sometimes worrying about those kinds of things. But more than that, I worry there's nothing to make the other person stay. Maybe that's irrational, but some part of me still feels anxious."

"Of course, I've never had an actual boyfriend yet," said Adam, "so I have to admit I don't know firsthand, but I don't think it would make a difference if someone had a little fun with other guys if they were serious about the other person."

Oliver seemed to consider this. Then he said, "I'm not sure I know what getting serious about another person would be like for me, or how I'd know, or how I'd feel if he had other boyfriends. Sorry, that sounds weird."

"No, not really." said Adam in a voice that sounded empathetic, but still somehow sadder than it might have. "I think it's okay to not know how you'd feel."

"So I think I want to say an open relationship would be okay, but I'm not sure. I'm sorry I can't be more definite about it."

Adam shrugged. "It's the way you feel."

"Yes."

"Here's another hypothetical, theoretical question, and I'm just asking so I understand you better. Do you actually want a boyfriend?"

"Yes, I do. Or at least I think I do. What about you?"

"I think I do too," said Adam.

The two of them sat in silence for a while, then Adam said, "I could sit in this one spot and never move again for the rest of my life."

"That's a long time."

"I don't care. I'm not getting up."

"You wanna go have dinner?"

"Yeah, let's go eat."

18

Evening pedestrian traffic on Haight was chaotic as usual when Randall met Adam on the sidewalk in front of All You Knead. They went inside and took a table in the middle of the restaurant near the aquarium where they could watch the goggle-eyed fancy goldfish wiggle around. After they ordered, Adam asked how Randall's interview went earlier in the day.

"It was for the manager of a consumer electronics store. I wouldn't make enough money, but they said there was potential for promotion to their corporate office. I think they meant it when they looked at my résumé. Who knows? They acted like they really wanted me but probably thought I was overqualified."

"Sounds crappy."

"Yeah, it does."

"How's yoga?"

"Yoga is pretty groovy. And there's this dude in the class I've been doing the nasty with. We met the first day and really hit it off."

"Is he from Nantucket?"

"He might as well be. But no, he's from Southern California.

And he's a bit of a New Ager. There's this line of products he's really into called... Earthy Luvin'."

"Ha! That's beautiful."

"I thought you might like that. Everything is either an antioxidant or an adaptogen. He's especially into their line of hair care. How you nourish hair with shampoo is beyond me since the part of it that you can wash doesn't have a blood supply, but what do I know? Anyway, the massage cream smells like coconut custard pie, so it can't all be baloney in a pill."

"Sounds harmless."

"Yeah, though the massage cream also makes you hungry. And you smell like a pie."

After their drinks arrived, Randall asked how things were going with Oliver.

"They're okay." Adam said it in a matter-of-fact way.

"It's nothing bad, I hope."

"No, or at least we didn't fight or anything. I'm having trouble knowing what I want from life right now—except fried mozzarella sticks."

Back at the apartment, Eugene had just come home from work to a package waiting in the lobby: a zentai suit. Of course, he had to rip open the bag immediately and check it out. He had chosen a steel blue one and made sure to include the crotch zipper. It looked pretty cool, and he would've tried it on immediately but something made him throw it in the wash first on the delicate setting. When he got back from the laundry room, he called Hector Guzmán.

"Hey Eugene!"

"Hey Superbear. Guess what I just got in the mail?"

"I'm guessing it would be a cosplay suit."

"That would be a correct guess. I'm washing it now, and I'm gonna let it drip dry."

"Wanna get together early next week and model it for me? Steve might be around but neither of us mind."

"I think he gets off on the idea of you and me knocking boots."

"Yeah, he does. So maybe Tuesday?"

"Tuesday's good."

"Do I get one of those massages?"

"You bet. Until then, Superbear."

After they hung up, Eugene put the phone in his pocket. A moment later took it out again and dialed Cody. It had been a while since they had seen each other. The call went to voice-mail. Eugene left a message, then started prepping his evening meal.

Over on Potrero Hill, Gustavo was hanging out in the living room, waiting for Jason to get home. It was one of his days off, and he had spent a good chunk of the time writing. Tom, one of the other roommates, was in the kitchen making dinner for himself. Gustavo had just put on some music and sat down to chill on the sofa when Jason came in, obviously unhappy.

It turned out that the company Jason worked for would soon be acquired by a bigger company in the South Bay.

"Unemployment would really suck right now," said Jason, taking off his shoes and sitting down on the other end of the sofa. "So would having to look for a job."

"Is there a chance they'd keep you on?"

"Maybe. But I don't wanna go down the Peninsula every day. I moved to San Francisco because I wanted to live here and not somewhere else. And I'd spend half my life on the train." Jason stretched out on the sofa. Gustavo moved closer and took Jason's feet in lap, massaging them as he removed the socks. Jason started to calm down.

"It's gonna be okay," Gustavo told him. "You'll find something in San Francisco if you want to. It'll be okay."

"Ugh. I just wanna forget about it right now. How was your day?"

"It was pretty nice. I worked on a story for a long time, which felt good. There's that party tonight for Orion's new boy if you wanna go."

"Not really," said Jason with a look of distaste.

Gustavo chuckled. "Yeah, me neither."

The Marty party had a good turnout at Molly's. A bunch of people were out front with cigarettes when Duane arrived, and he stood away from them to avoid the smoke. He didn't have to wait long before Seth showed up, greeting Duane with a hug. Inside, Orion was holding court at the corner of the bar with Marty, who was standing nearby but slightly out of reach. He was wearing the usual black outfit minus the shades, not that it made much difference. His bandmates were scattered around the room, drinking and playing pool. Seth noticed the peroxided front man and gave him the eye.

"Hey, those are the guys who played the first set when I ran into you on Punk Night," Duane said. "I think the longhair's Marty. The friend I was with knows him too."

"Oh gawd—that night," Seth recalled. "Anyway, yeah, you're right. I don't know why I didn't put it together before. There's the sexy one with the fucked-up hair. I thought he looked familiar."

"What do you think of Marty?"

"He would be good looking if he didn't have the facial expression of an ashtray. Maybe Orion's slipping. Whatever. I guess I'll go say hello."

Orion was in the middle of saying something about how he was introducing Swapped Condoms to some very interesting

people. In the '70s, he used to hang out with Jon Frame from
Gemme Fingerbøl. When he noticed Seth, Orion leaned
forward on his barstool for a hug.

"This is my friend Duane," said Seth. Orion made sure to
check Duane out as they shook hands.

"Have you met Marty?" Orion said. Duane looked at Orion's
latest protégé. There was a bland prettiness to the features. The
sleeveless t-shirt showed a tight little boyish body, skinny but
not excessively so. He definitely had a certain appeal, though it
was hard to get past the flatness of affect, literally. Seth was
right. Marty had the personality of an ashtray.

After a few minutes of chatter, Seth turned to Duane and
suggested they go get a drink. They went to the well, and Seth
ordered a gin and tonic. Duane got a beer. When they were far
enough away not to be overheard, Duane said, "Orion is pretty
sure of his own greatness."

"He's obscene. He really does make some interesting pieces,
though. And he's good at the biz because he somehow gets
people to do things for him. He's just one of those people. It's
disgusting. I met him in this class he taught as a visiting artist
in Chicago about ten years ago. He was drooling on me the
whole time."

"That sounds… slobbery," said Duane.

"I should have had a fucking umbrella."

Duane laughed. "So how have you been? I haven't seen you
since that night. And here we are at another Swapped
Condoms event!"

"I know. I seem to be going from swapped condom to
swapped condom. Things are so stressful right now. I'm
supposed to go to L.A. for this show. It's a really big deal for me
but I don't feel like going all the way down there. And I'll have
to rent a fucking car. Whatever. L.A. is obnoxious but then San
Francisco these days is pretty obnoxious too. Anyway, how are
you? You look really good."

"Thanks," said Duane. "I'm doing okay. I need to look for a job."

"That's such a drag."

"Yeah, I didn't want to have to think about it right now. Anyway, I'm trying to decide what I'll do next. It would be great to do something creative. On the other hand, I could just stop thinking about any of that for a while and clean houses or something."

"Would you really clean houses? That's so exploitive. You can do better than that."

"I don't think it's exploitive. I like working with my hands, and I'd get paid in cash."

"You're a smart, creative person. You should be using that."

"Maybe. Anyway, I don't know if I'd really clean houses. It was just the first thing that came into my head. But I'm wondering if maybe I should move back to Maryland."

"Would you really?" Seth said it like Duane might be moving back to the primordial ooze.

"Well, my family's there."

"Are you close to your family?"

"Yeah, I am. And it's funny but you can tell we're related because we have a similar aesthetic. We like the same things visually."

"That's really cool. I wish mine were like that. Unfortunately, their unifying trait is neuroticism. I try to avoid dealing with them whenever I can. With my luck, they'll all live a million years so they can drive me insane." Seth took a sip of his drink. "Sorry. I'm so stressed out about this L.A. trip. Everything's been really fucked up lately, and now I have to go to L.A."

"Somehow, I've never been there," said Duane.

"It's a pit. And it's huge. It goes on forever."

"Well, I hope your show is a success." Changing the subject, Duane said, "Hey, you know how you said I should explore my sexuality in my art? I've decided I'm gonna shoot portraits of bikers."

"Bikers? That's so sleazy."

"I dunno, maybe some of them. But they're interesting and have lots of personality, and I think they're sexy."

"That's just so... you want to have sex with bikers?"

"Well, not all of 'em, but maybe some. Why not?"

This was too much for Seth. "I'm picturing some huge guy in sweaty leather and denim."

"Yeah, that's the idea," said Duane, amused.

Seth saw some people he knew and wanted to go talk to them. So Duane went along, but Seth's friends weren't making any effort to include him. He excused himself, saying he was going to check out the pool table.

A short, dark-haired woman was just finishing a game with the peroxided front man from Swapped Condoms as Duane walked up to them. The front man, whose name was Chris, shook hands with his opponent, who then wandered off, and there was no one else waiting. Chris had a sweet smile. He was wearing a flannel shirt with cut-off sleeves over a white undershirt, and the hair in his pits showed when he leaned over to take a shot. Duane played extra carefully. It was all very flirty.

After a while, Seth came over to watch. When Duane had finished his game, he and Seth got another drink, then people-watched a while longer.

"Marty doesn't actually talk, does he?" said Duane.

"He doesn't need to. Orion does all the talking for the both of them."

"Do you think Orion's doing him?"

"Maybe," said Seth, "though it's hard to imagine Marty having sex with anybody at all."

"I dunno," said Duane with a snerk, "Marty could just lie there."

"Maybe they frot or something," Seth laughed. "Sorry, that's really gross."

Duane watched as Chris and some of his friends left the bar.

"It feels like it's winding down a little," Duane said.

"Yeah, I was thinking about going pretty soon, but don't feel like you need to leave with me."

"I think I'm done here too. Wanna go to my place?"

"I really just want to go home, if that's okay. I hope you don't feel like I'm abandoning you."

"No, it's totally fine."

"Thanks. I feel like I need to hide under the covers for a while."

They found Seth a cab, and Duane started to walk home.

After a block and a half, he turned around and started toward the leather bars instead. He could look for bikers to photograph, even if it was just to chat them up and give out his number or something.

Duane didn't really know if any bikers were to be found hanging out and having a drink that evening, but he picked a spot that seemed as likely as any and went inside. The place was moderately busy. A few seats were open at the bar, so Duane sat down and ordered a beer. He took a sip and twisted around on the barstool to check out the room.

"King of all he surveys," said a suave voice next to him. Duane looked to see who had spoken and saw a stunning man of about fifty, with chiseled features and well-groomed salt and pepper hair, wearing a pewter-grey dress shirt and a charcoal jacket. He was drinking a brilliant, frosty, translucent jade green drink in a stemmed glass, lit from above the bar.

"Hi, I'm Perry."

Duane hesitated, then introduced himself.

"Duane, you look like a really intelligent person. I can see it in your eyes."

"Thank you," said Duane awkwardly. This guy was not a biker or anything even close to the sort of clientele Duane should've expected to find in a bar like that. It wasn't clear what Perry was doing there at all, let alone why he was talking to Duane, apart from the intelligent look in Duane's eyes.

"This is just a guess," said Perry, "but you look like you do some type of creative work."

It was all oddly frank. Perry had a certain disquieting magnetism, but he seemed harmless enough. Duane answered that, yeah, he was sort of an artist in a minor way, adding he worked in a photo equipment sales and rental shop.

"I could tell by the way you looked around the room. You made a critical assessment of your surroundings."

"Um, yeah, at the moment, I'm looking for models for a photo series I'm thinking about."

"Excellent. I have no doubt that you'll find those models. Do you have a card?"

"No, not yet."

"You should have a card. Who do you want to photograph?"

"I'm, um, thinking about bikers."

"Great subject! I don't even have to see your stuff, and I can tell you right now that project is gonna be terrific. Get a card. Listen, I have to go, but it was really good running into you. Maybe I'll see your bikers sometime soon. Keep doing exactly what you're doing, but get that card."

And with that, Perry quaffed his green drink and walked off into the night.

19

THE NEXT DAY, Duane arrived at Hengist a quarter of an hour early with a package of laser printer business card paper from the stationery store a few blocks away on Market. When Randall came in, Duane told him about what had happened the night before.

"Are you sure he wasn't trying to hit on you?"

"At first, I wondered if he might be, even though it didn't seem like it, just because I couldn't figure out why the heck he was talking to me. But I'm pretty sure it wasn't a come on. And the weirdest part was the drink."

"You said it was bright green and in a cocktail glass?"

"Yeah. I'd never seen anything like it."

"It sounds like a Grasshopper."

"A Grasshopper?"

"A creamy chocolate-mint concoction favored by my great-aunt Alma."

Duane laughed. "A guy like that?!"

"Well, maybe not, but you never know."

"In a leather bar?"

"You said he was confident."

Randall unlocked the front door. In a few minutes, they had customers, but the usual energy had been lacking ever since Hengist had announced it was going out of business at the end of the month. Lots of people had been coming in for bargains and to have a last look or two at what had been a local institution.

Richard had seen the news about Hengist in the paper. Another independent retail anchor was gone, or would be soon. He looked through the windows of his office suite at the city below, at an ugly new tower in one spot and a massive construction site in another. Soon they would all be filled with kids like Dustin who had no idea what city they were moving to or why. It was already full of them. Richard's team had an interview with another one at eleven. Maybe he wouldn't be too awful.

At ground level across the street, Jason stood in line at a coffee outlet. He didn't need more caffeine at that moment, but reaching for it was automatic, reflexive. He was extra early for an interview that morning because he didn't dare be late. Or jittery. When he got to the front of the queue to place his order, he chose sparkling water instead.

He still had some time to kill, so he tooled around downtown trying not to get too sweaty. He navigated the busy sidewalks full of people, all on anonymous errands of their own in the hive of downtown. All in motion, purposeful, intent, going somewhere to do something they were required to do. It was like limbo, something between feeling and not feeling, their real personalities and experiences on pause for eight or more hours of an android-like state of being they endured five days a week, yet the whole point of living in San Francisco was to be more alive.

Jason checked the time, then headed toward the address he had written down for the interview. Suddenly, he giggled to himself. He didn't even know if this job would be right for him, and it didn't matter. He walked confidently into the lobby and took the elevator to the sixth floor. He didn't even know if he'd like the people. Or working for this company. When the elevator doors opened again, a guy was standing directly in front of them, blocking the way. Jason laughed at that too.

That evening, Lacey's was packed for another open mic. Some people had remembered Randall from the last time, and he got some whistles and cheers as he went up to the front of the room.

"Thank you, everyone. It's good to be here tonight. I call this one 'Pod People.'"

Ever since the invasion two weeks before by beings from a distant planet, Roger had been pissed off. Ordinary, respectable humans were slowly being replaced by facsimiles: creatures that looked in every way like real humans except they were on earth to create havoc. What they were up to no one could tell because mostly they were doing nothing at all, and it was driving the few remaining real people like Roger absolutely crazy.

"Well, there's *a fine howdy do! Now we have an extraterrestrial invasion. Okay, so we have one. But what's the point of it all? They just sit around! I haven't even seen a single ray gun! They just stand around looking like real people only stupider and get in your way! Some invasion! Hell, you can't even get probed!"*

Roger wanted to know who was in charge. Didn't any of those space people know how to run their operation? For all he could tell, there were a few big shots riding around in their fancy antigravity cars. What good were they? Roger half-admired their nerve, but he knew he wasn't going to get a chance at being able to ride one of those cars. He was being treated like a peasant like everyone else, and he was mad about it, all right.

He picked up the phone and called directory assistance for the police department.

"No, it's not an emergency! But it's—it's, look, it's urgent, okay? Well how in the world am I supposed to know?! I'm the one calling Information!"

He got the non-emergency number and dialed it, but the police told him there was no law on the books against doing nothing.

"I can't believe this! There must be someone I can talk to! You're under the control of those space aliens!"

The police wished him a good day and hung up. Dammit, he'd call the governor's office. He'd call the Pentagon. But for all Roger knew, they were all under the control of the extraterrestrials. Probably they had been replaced too.

"Nuts to this!"

Roger drove to the supermarket to buy groceries. But instead of the consumer goods he might have in all decency expected to find, it was full of useless items no one in their right mind would care to buy. He went up to a clerk and said, "Excuse me but can you please help me find the oat bran?"

The clerk told him that it was in Aisle 4.

"I looked in Aisle 4 and there is no oat bran."

The clerk accompanied Roger to Aisle 4, and sure enough, there was no oat bran, as if Roger couldn't see that for himself. The clerk said he would look to see if they had any in the back.

"Would you, please?"

Roger waited a very long time.

"Damned extraterrestrials!"

The clerk eventually returned and told Roger he was very sorry but they had no oat bran. He might check back Thursday.

"Hah—Thursday!"

Roger wheeled his cart to the cashier, cursing to himself.

"No oat bran till Thursday. What the hell is this? First there's an invasion of space people, now you can't get oat bran until Thursday."

Roger paid and took his groceries to his car. On the way home, he *devised a plan to grow his own food. That would show them. No oat bran, indeed. He carried the groceries into the house and put them away, made a whisky sour and sat down in front of the television. There was nothing on. Every channel was playing some damned commercial or something.*

The phone rang. It was his sister Irene. She said she was fine though it was hot in Ohio. Arthur was fine. He said it was too hot to mow the lawn.

"And how's Terry? Uh-huh. He's a space alien?! Oh, I see. Well, yes, I know things are different nowadays. Well, does he do anything? Okay, well I suppose that's the way it is. Yes, I know. I guess his girlfriend's the same, is she?'

Irene said that she believed so.

"Say, listen, do you suppose Terry knows anything about how to get one of those antigravity cars?"

20

BEFORE HENGIST OPENED for the day, Duane gave Randall one of his new cards. "Is it a business card if I can't actually pay the models?"

"Yes," said Randall, "and maybe you'll be able to pay them one day soon. So how are you gonna find bikers?"

"I was wondering. There's the bar where I met Perry. I'm also thinking about that coffee place that for some reason is popular with bears."

"Oh yeah, the bear café! That might be just the place. You'd get way less drunk waiting around for models, too."

Duane laughed. "I hadn't thought about it that way. I might just head there after work sometime this week, though I don't know if I have time today. At some point, I need to do laundry. I'm just about out of clean clothes."

"Ah yes, the sock problem. Sometimes I just buy more. It pretty much guarantees you don't run out."

"You have anything going on tonight?"

"Dinner with Adam and Eugene. I'm bringing Nature Boy."

"That sounds like fun."

"I hope it will be. Maybe they'll like him."

. . .

That evening, Adam and Eugene were on the back patio of a restaurant on the north side of Haight near Cole where Randall and Drew were supposed to join them. Adam looked at his phone. "They just found a parking spot."

"So, he met this guy in a yoga class at the gym?"

"Yeah. He works in some hydroponic store."

"I wonder if he grows weed."

"Probably. Anyway, I take it he and Randall ball like baboons in a tree."

A few moments later, Randall and Drew arrived on the patio, and Randall made introductions. Drew's unbleached cotton Guatemalan shirt was open at the top and showed off the pretty little recess where his clavicles met his sternum.

They sat down and Adam said, "I like your shirt."

"Thank you!" Drew gushed. "It's really comfortable."

"Your pants look really comfortable too," said Eugene.

"They are. I like to be unconfined."

"Yes," said Randall, "pants are often so inhibiting."

Everyone agreed. The server came over, but they needed more time with the menu. He told them he'd come back.

"Should we get a pitcher of sangria?" suggested Randall.

Drew loved sangria.

"Yes, let's do that," said Adam.

Eugene suggested they get an appetizer. Drew loved appetizers. They decided on spinach empanadillas. In a little while, the server returned and took their order.

"So, Drew," said Adam, "Randall said you work in a plant store?"

"Yes, on Market in the Castro. I'm also helping some friends of mine market a line of personal care products and supplements they've started called Earthy Luvin'."

Eugene grinned but managed to say calmly, "What kinds of products do they make?"

Drew gave the names of powders, capsules, energy drinks, moisturizers, shampoo, conditioner, exfoliants, and aphrodisiacs, all of which had been compounded from herbal substances used for healing since ancient times.

The sangria arrived.

"I hear sangria can be used as a healing substance," said Randall.

"Yes," concurred Adam, "I believe you're right."

"Oh, definitely!" said Drew with a sly smile.

While Randall poured the drinks, Eugene asked Drew what his favorite Earthy Luvin' product was.

"The hair care products are wonderful. Good hair care is so important."

"You have really great hair," said Adam.

"Thank you. But maybe if I had to pick one favorite product, I'd say the Chili-Cacao Mojo Cocoa."

"I've had that one," said Randall, "and I have to say it's very tasty. It's a little piquant too. It's... good for getting your toes warm."

"And it helps increase circulation to *all* your extremities," Drew added.

"Well!" said Adam, "that sounds like something anyone might enjoy."

"I could get you some Mojo Cocoa," Drew offered suggestively. It sounded like Drew knew exactly what Adam could do with his mojo.

Adam smiled. "Maybe I'll take you up on that."

"You guys are from New York?" Drew asked.

"Yeah," said Eugene, "we're staying in a sublet through the end of September."

"That's awesome! I've always wanted to go to New York."

"Well, you could think of tonight as a preview," said Adam.

"We could give you your own taste of New York, couldn't we, Eugene?"

"Yeah, like a personal tour."

Drew thought that sounded amazing.

Their appetizers came, and Drew proclaimed them delicious. Everything was awesome. The restaurant was really great. San Francisco had so many amazing places.

"You should see the sublet these guys scored," said Randall.

"Yeah," said Adam, exchanging glances with Eugene. "Maybe later, we can all take a look at it."

"Yeah, if you have time after dinner, we'd be happy to show it to you," said Eugene.

"That would be great!" Drew looked carefully at Eugene. "I think I recognize you. You're a trainer at the gym, aren't you?"

"That's right."

"This guy gives the most amazing massages," said Randall.

"I'll bet!" said Drew.

At the end of the meal, the server came by and asked if they would like any dessert or coffee, but they were all too full. He said he'd bring the check.

Adam said, "Hey Eugene, whaddya say we invite these guys for a little dessert at our place?"

After they paid, they went over to the other side of the Panhandle in Randall's van. He had to circle a few times for a spot, but it wasn't too bad. When they got inside, they went into the living room and Adam pushed the coffee table out of the way.

Eugene said, "Drew, would you like a massage?"

At a little after eleven, Adam and Eugene said goodnight to Randall and Drew. Drew had been the guest of honor, though Eugene had used his therapeutic talents to beat the tension out of Randall as well.

"That was fun," said Adam. They were in the kitchen. Eugene sat beside the table. Adam was pouring himself a glass of water from the sink.

"Yeah, it was. Drew's a moon child, but he's fun to play with and he's nice. He really takes care of his body, too, though Randall's in better condition than I would've thought. Must be the swimming and surfing."

"I loved the sounds of agony when you worked on Randall's neck and shoulders."

"Heheh—he's got some tight muscles there, for sure." Eugene laced his fingers and stretched his arms in front of him. "Arright—I'm gonna go to bed. I have an appointment with Steve in the morning. I'm thinking about inviting myself to go hiking with him and Hector."

"Do they have a car?"

"Yeah. They have some indestructible old hatchback. There's a place they like to hike way south of here that has caves and turkey vultures."

"Sounds cool. Have you heard from Cody lately?"

"Nope. That boy has vanished."

21

"Heya Ted!" Gustavo came walking toward him from the back of the store with a price sticker gun in his hand. Ted had been browsing the staff picks, looking at a book Gustavo had written up. "That one's really good," Gustavo said.

"Then I'll get it," Ted said, carrying it to the counter. "So how was the open mic? I'm sorry I couldn't make it."

"It was great. There's this dude I met in the seminar this summer who read a crazy social satire about an invasion from outer space."

"Gee, now I'm doubly sorry I missed it. Do I know the guy?"

"Maybe. Randall DeVries?"

"Oh yeah, he took my class. Really imaginative. Aw, what a shame to have missed that. It must've been a fun piece."

"It was a total blast. He read something good at the previous open mic too. And he's a really nice guy. He gave me and my boyfriend a ride home each time at the end of the night. Jason is always nodding out by the time we're done because he's coming right from a long day at work."

Ted smiled a funny smile and said, "I didn't know you had a

boyfriend. That's wonderful, Gustavo. How long have you been together?"

"We met late last fall. We've been living together since March."

"How wonderful. He's a lucky guy to have you."

"I'm lucky to have *him*. He's one of the sweetest, most caring people I've ever met. He's always thinking of things that would make me happy. I hope I'm as good to him as he is to me."

"That's beautiful, Gustavo. Really, it is. I wish you both all the happiness in the world together."

Out in the Avenues, Randall and Drew were conducting an experiment in cohabitation on a temporary basis. One of Drew's hosts in the Mission was expecting a visit from his mother, and Drew needed to make different plans for a week. Randall had agreed to let him camp out for a while and had lent him a key.

Drew didn't have a lot of stuff to move, but some of it was very smoky. On his first day at Randall's, Drew came back from the plant shop and went through the apartment with a small, tightly bound bundle of smoldering herbs, performing a ritual of purification.

In the middle of this, Randall returned from Hengist holding an untidy clutch of mail. "Something smells like a burning sofa."

"Sorry, I'm just smudging!" Drew said. "Wherever I stay, I do this thing to align myself with the energies present in the home. It'll just take a minute. I'm finishing up right now."

Randall watched this for a few seconds, then said, "I'm just going to aid in the banishment of negative energies by opening the windows."

He put down his briefcase, dropped the mail on top of a larger pile on the desk, and started letting some fresh air into the room. He went to the bathroom, opened that window too, urinated, then went to the kitchen to open up the window in there. On the counter were many vegetables.

"You bought groceries."

Drew came from the other room with his smudge stick, tamping it out in a little brass bowl.

"I'd like to make dinner as a thank you gift for letting me stay here for a few days."

"Gee, you didn't have to do that."

Randall picked up a roundish, light brown tuber.

"That's jícama!" Drew said gleefully. He pronounced it *HEE-cah-mah*.

"So that's what it looks like. How long do we have before dinner?"

"We can eat whenever you want."

"Sounds good. I was thinking about taking a shower first."

"Okay."

"Would you like to join me?"

"Sure!"

A certain coffee outlet in the Castro was for some reason popular with burlier, more hirsute fellows. When Duane arrived, the place was slow. He ordered a large half-caff, chatted with the barista, and sat down to what seemed like an improbable stakeout for bikers. There wasn't a lot of business at that moment, but the bland art on the wall provided some diversion at least until he finished his coffee.

Suddenly, a husky, handsome, bearded young man in leathers with the patch of a gay motorcycle club on his jacket and a helmet under his arm bellied up to the counter and ordered a depth charge. Duane watched him with casual interest as he waited for his order. He looked just like Duane's notion of a biker.

Duane scrambled to his feet, patted his pockets, found his wallet, dug out his card and almost ran over to the guy.

"Hi there, my name's Duane." He smiled and started to put out a hand to shake, then pressed his sweaty palm to his jeans. The guy was very big in every direction. "I'm an amateur photographer, and I'm doing a series of biker portraits. I wonder if maybe you'd like to sit for me. I can't pay anything, but I'd be happy to share the photos with you."

"Hey man, nice to meet you! That sounds like a great project." The guy had a loud voice. "I'm a photographer too. My name's Jack. Yeah, sure, I'd model for you. Maybe you'd be interested in photographing me with my boyfriend? I'm pretty sure he'd be into it." Jack had a friendly smile, even if he was a bit scary.

"That would be—that would be just great."

"I might know other guys who'd like to model for you, too. You look sort of familiar. Do you ride?"

"I, um, I haven't actually been on a motorcycle," Duane said, looking like he might sink into the ground, "but if you're a photographer, you might recognize me from my job. I work at Hengist, at least for the moment."

"That must be where I know you! Man, it's a shame that store's going away. Hey, are you looking for a job? I work for a commercial photography studio and they're looking for an intern. I think it's only twenty hours a week. I'm sure it doesn't pay much, but they do high quality work."

Duane and Jack exchanged cards.

After dinner, Adam and Eugene went out for a drink and a game of pool. The bar was only moderately busy and not too loud. A dude sitting at the end near the pool table looked at Adam frequently. A wolf-like dog with silvery fur sat at his feet.

Adam had just taken some trouble with what turned out to

be an unsatisfactory shot when he said, "What do you think of the guy with the dog?"

Eugene casually glanced over that direction: boyish, fashion-model handsome, mixed race, pretty eyes, medium height, graceful body.

"So fine."

"I agree. He's been giving me the eye."

"You gonna go for him?"

"Yeah, I believe I am. You don't mind?"

"Not at all. Enjoy."

After they wrapped up the game and Eugene took off, Adam went over to the beauty who had been glancing over in his direction for the last ten minutes.

"Is this seat open?"

"It sure is, mister."

"Out by yourself?"

"Yeah, sometimes when I walk Misty here," scratching the dog's head, "I stop for a drink."

"You live around here?"

"Yeah. Me and my two boyfriends live on Page."

It caught Adam by surprise. He asked with a grin, "What do they call that—a throuple?"

The beautiful stranger laughed. "Yeah, a throuple. My name's Gary, by the way."

"Mine's Adam. Nice to meet you. Can I buy you another beer?"

"I should get going."

"Can I walk you and Misty somewhere?"

"Yeah, sure."

When they were outside, Adam said, "Do you need to go right home?"

"No, not right home. Misty would enjoy a longer walk."

They finished their drinks and headed out into the night

air. Gary steered them toward a quieter side street where Misty could take her time sniffing at the trees.

"So what's it like being in a throuple?" Adam asked.

Gary was amused by the question and looked like he was trying to decide how to respond. "They're great guys. We've made a wonderful home together."

They walked in silence for a moment, then Adam said, "Do you ever have boyfriends on the side?"

"Not really, no."

"Is it off limits?"

"Not exactly."

"Would you like to come back to my place for a little while?"

"I—I would, but I just can't. You're very cute, though."

"So are you."

They waited for a light to change, then crossed the street, turning left. The air was still and the fog made halos around the electric lights. Soon they were standing in front of a small apartment house. Gary looked at Adam longingly.

"This is where we live."

"Are you sure I can't talk you into coming home with me for just a little while?"

Gary hesitated. He smiled sadly. "I can't."

"Oh well. You're really sexy, man."

"Thanks. So are you. Have a good night."

"Thanks. You too."

When Eugene got home from the bar, he called Hector to see if he and Steve wanted to go to Carmel Valley a week from Sunday. It was already after ten thirty.

"I'm not disturbing you, am I?"

"Nah," said Hector. "We live on adult entertainment time."

"That's what I figured. So can I talk you guys into driving us almost three hours away to walk in the heat and dust?"

"Yeah, when were you thinking about?"

"A week from Sunday."

Hector checked with Steve, and a week from Sunday was fine.

"Great," said Eugene. "I guess we can work out the details when we get close to the date. Anyway, how are you guys doing?"

"Pretty good. We shot a great scene this afternoon in the ground floor playroom of some guys our business partner knows. It's quite a setup. It opens onto a garden deck with a hot tub and tropical plants and stuff, but we didn't show that part. Just the playroom."

"Sounds wild."

"We have major house envy. Anyway, how're you?"

"I'm okay. I had dinner with Adam. Then we went for a couple of drinks and a game of pool. Some dude was checking him out, so I made myself scarce."

"You wanna come over?"

"I want to but I have a seven a.m. client. I'd better call it a night or I'll be dragging."

"Well if you change your mind, I'll be up for a while."

Eugene got off the phone and went to the bathroom to take out his contacts. The front door lock turned and Adam came in, going to the kitchen to get a glass of water. He was alone, so Eugene joined him.

"Looks like it didn't work out." Eugene poured himself a glass of water too.

"It was weird. The guy was obviously into me but he was in a committed three-way relationship and couldn't tear himself away. I got the idea it was allowed, but he was the one holding himself back. We walked around a while with the dog, then I walked him to his door. I offered to bring him back here for a quickie, but he wouldn't go for it."

"That *is* weird. And too bad. A three-way relationship, huh?"

"Yeah. Must be interesting."

"Come to think of it, I almost have that now, but not exactly."

"Yeah, not exactly."

"Sort of a special friend of the family."

"They could introduce you that way at parties. 'And this is Eugene, a special friend of the family.'"

"If anyone asked how I was special, I could offer to show them sometime."

22

RANDALL HAD JUST BEEN to a less than optimal job interview at a photo printing and framing shop. From the moment the store manager laid eyes on him, he felt he was being endured like something peeled off the bottom of a shoe. And it had cost too much to pay for parking. Randall hadn't liked the place all that much anyway, but his gameness should've spoken for good faith and character. When he let himself into his apartment, Drew wasn't home yet. He was alone at last.

"Fuck 'em all."

He took off his interview clothes and sat down at the desk to space out in front of the computer in his t-shirt and underwear.

At that moment, he heard a sound outside the apartment. Drew had returned. When the door opened, Randall didn't look up.

"Hi! I'm back!"

Drew had a plant with him. It was spiky and vertical.

"I brought you a plant! It's a dracaena." Drew pronounced it *druh-SEE-nuh*. He was saying something about the plant and the store that day. It wasn't a bad plant, really, though it would need to be looked after. At least it sounded like maybe it was an easy plant to keep.

"Thank you. That's very thoughtful. Maybe we should put it in the kitchen window."

"I think that would be enough light," said Drew, taking the plant with him.

Randall closed his eyes. When he opened them again, Drew was on the futon with his laptop.

"I think it'll be perfect in there!" Drew said airily.

Sitting on the desk was a pizzeria menu that had been stuck through the slats of the garden gate. Randall picked it up and perused the options. There were some coupons. If he ordered a large, they could have dinner and maybe Randall would still have some of it for breakfast the next day.

"Oh wow!" Drew was checking email. "I got my report from Mineral Testing Innovations!"

"Sound exciting. What's Mineral Testing Innovations?"

"They do hair analysis. It tells you all about your health, your diet, toxicity, and all kinds of other things based on the metals in your body."

"You don't say?"

"This is fabulous," said Drew as he scrolled through a forty-page PDF. "There's so much information here." He went back to the summary near the beginning. "It says I'm the Upsilon Type."

"What does that mean?"

"I don't know yet. But it looks like I have a natural tendency toward some kind of mineral dysregulation. It also means I tend to have a strong pancreas, bile duct, and duodenum. I have a strong pineal gland."

"I've always believed that everyone has a special gift."

"I have a tendency toward electromagnetic hypersensitivity." Drew looked slightly concerned. "I have a deficit of chromium, which could indicate adrenal fatigue and autointox-ication."

"Is that when you get drunk by yourself?"

Drew suddenly became wide-eyed. "Oh my gawd—I have all these mineral imbalances! I have elevated levels of fluorine, vanadium and strontium... they're saying that's something called Toxic Hair!"

He was scrolling through the report, transfixed.

"Maybe if I do a juice cleanse...."

Randall set aside the pizza menu and folded his hands in his lap. "There is no such thing as toxic hair. There is no such thing as a fucking juice cleanse. This is one hundred percent, straight up horseshit. I'm not even going to ask what you paid for this so-called report. Hair is just hair, okay? There is nothing wrong with you."

"There's nothing wrong with me?" said Drew confusedly. Randall got next to him on the futon and put his hand on Drew's shoulder.

"You're twenty-four years old and in better health than most people on earth. You do yoga and eat organic fucking vegetables. This is horseshit. What if some random report told you that in the next twenty-four hours, your entrails will fall out of your asshole?"

Drew had to admit that maybe it did sound unlikely.

"Horse shit," Randall repeated more gently. "Now, do you like green peppers on your pizza? They won't give you toxic hair but they may repeat on you."

It was early, but the morning light coming through the bay window of Adam's room somehow made him push off the covers and jump in the shower.

In the kitchen, Eugene was washing his breakfast dishes. Adam said to him, "I'm gonna walk to work today."

So he strolled out the door in that general direction, bouncing around the other pedestrians on Divisadero, zigzagging down the sidewalk like a bee. Cars strained at stop signs, edging corners, crowding intersections, frustrated people stalled in hassle machines, mammoths stuck in the tar.

"Today I am the bus."

He zipped through the Lower Haight, humming across Duboce Park, passing dozy dog walkers and kids in strollers. People stood waiting for the N Judah. A crow cawed and Adam cawed back.

At Sanchez, he turned east at 14th Street, rolling on down to ford the river of Market by the big supermarket sign. While stopped at a red light at Dolores, the wide street beckoned to him with its long meridian of cool Canary Island palms. But the signal changed, and down Adam went till 14th flattened to the level of downtown. Traffic congestion eased and cleared, and he was surrounded by an abstract industrial landscape that told him he was approaching Harrison Street, and that he was most of the way there.

When he turned onto Mariposa, he had time for one brief pause, so he took a few minutes to buy a cup of coffee, then ambled through the front door of CUE and into the MFA office.

Delma looked up and sat back in her chair.

"You're in a good mood," she observed.

"I just walked to work."

"You must be exhausted!"

"Not really."

"Was there some reason you did this?"

"I just felt like it."

"He just *felt* like it."

Ted came out of his office.

"Hey Adam, got a sec?"

"Yeah, sure."

Adam took his coffee in with him and closed the door.

"Just so you know, it's nothing bad," Ted said. "You've been a great addition to the office this summer, and we would be able to extend you through the end of September, if you want."

This was good news. They had about a month left in the sublet, and while Adam hadn't been spending much money, he really could've used more. He gratefully accepted Ted's offer.

"Good, I'm glad," said Ted. "We'll be very happy to have you for another month."

"Hey Ted, can I ask you something?"

"Of course. What's on your mind?"

"Do you think you'll be able to post that student services manager job anytime soon?"

"The dean's office has asked me to hold off for a little while. Can we talk about it again in a couple of weeks?"

Adam said that would be fine.

At around noon, Adam met Randall in the café after the latter had gone to yet another interview. Randall ordered at the counter and came back with an Italian soda and a number on a metal stand. He flopped down in his chair.

"Drew is completely batshit."

"Oh no."

"Oh yes. I can't wait for him to leave. It was supposed to have been a couple of days ago. I have this almost over-whelming dread that I'll never get rid of him."

"Man, that's miserable. I thought you guys were having fun."

"It was okay at first, though he's not the brightest light in the harbor. And my fridge is full of things I don't recognize. Then it turned out that he had bought some crackpot hair analysis report, and they came back with several yards of fake diagnoses about made-up health conditions. He totally believed it."

"Holy crap!"

"Eventually, I got him to calm down and we ordered a pizza. I think it was the first thing he'd eaten in days that wasn't mostly made from kale."

"So has he told you when he plans to leave?"

"He was supposed to go back to the two guys he had been staying with before someone's mother came for a visit, but they told him they needed a little time after she left to be by themselves. I can't imagine they'd be thrilled to put up with him either, which has me worried, but it sounds like they have a lot more space."

"Can't he stay in a hotel or something?"

"Maybe he could, but I'd feel bad kicking him out."

"Maybe you could find an excuse, like you want your life back. But I bet he won't hang around too much longer. It'll be fine."

"I hope you're right."

"How did the interview go? You're not as dressed up today."

"This place is more casual. It's across the Bay in Emeryville, which would cost me in gas mileage, but it's also a little more hands-on and thoughtful with the film processing than some of the other places I've been looking, which is one of the things I like about working at Hengist. And they sound pretty relaxed about letting the staff use their darkroom if it doesn't get in the way of company business."

"That sounds like a good perk."

"Yeah, it could be a pretty nice job if I could work on my own stuff a little. That reminds me—did I tell you Duane has this portrait project? It looks like it's starting to come together."

The exterior of the one-story building didn't give much away. It was one of a few commercial spaces scattered through the residential blocks at the southern end of Potrero Hill. It looked well cared for. Duane rang the doorbell, waited about half a minute, and was buzzed in. He was carrying a black portfolio he had just bought the day before. The reception area was lit mostly by a skylight, with a few large-format photos on the walls. The studio was a remodeled auto body shop. It looked expensive.

A trim guy in his forties wearing a grey sweater that looked like cashmere came out and introduced himself as Alec. He was energetic and cheerful with an edge just beneath the surface. Duane was smiling too much. Alec led him back to the main space, a large, open area which was set up for portrait photography. Another guy was moving some gear around. He stopped for second and waved.

"That's Paul, my partner," said Alec. "Come, let's talk over here."

One corner was arranged as an office with cabinets, drawers, and desks. Duane's portfolio was outclassed by the furniture. Alec motioned toward some low armchairs near a coffee table. "So you know Jack?"

"Yeah, we met in a café, and I gave him my card because I thought he'd be a good model for a project of mine."

"That's wonderful! I see you brought your portfolio with you. I hope you don't mind, but I'm gonna put you on the spot right away and ask to take a look."

Duane said that would be great.

Duane had chosen twenty images for his portfolio, among which were a whopping total of two bikers, one of which was Nick, Jack's boyfriend. The biker photos were first and last, like bookends. Unfortunately, Duane didn't have twenty stellar portraits, so he threw in a couple of other studio-lit images shot in a similar way.

Assuming Alec even liked Duane's padded portfolio, the photos on the walls were classy but conventional. The internship might have been more interesting had it paid enough for Duane to support himself, and he didn't know what sort of second job he could find to make up the difference. He was talented in lots of ways, but couldn't have said, if asked, that he was passionate about any of them.

"Hey, that's Nick!" Alec said, lighting up. He had recognized Jack's boyfriend from the portrait.

Duane was startled at first by the reaction, then smiled.

"Yeah, I guess it makes sense you'd know him."

"This is a beautiful image. Hey Paul! You gotta see this!"

23

ADAM AND EUGENE decided to live in San Francisco.

They let the idea sink in for a couple of days before breaking the news to their families. Eugene thought his parents would probably be disappointed he was moving so far away, but they'd handle the news well. Adam wasn't so sure about his mother because he was the baby of the family. But when he dialed Bay Ridge, Marleen said she had wondered if San Francisco might be calling to him.

"Is it okay?"

"Hey, I'm your mother. I want you to be happy."

After he got off the phone, Adam went into the kitchen to find Eugene, who asked how it went.

"If she was dying inside, she wouldn't tell me."

"Maybe she is, but she wants you to be happy."

"That's exactly what she said."

"No wonder she likes me."

"What about your folks?"

"They're already planning their first visit."

"Ha! Excellent. I hope they don't expect us to put them up. I get the feeling our next place is gonna be the size of a shoebox."

"Yeah, probably. Anyway, it feels good to have that conversation out of the way."

"Yeah, though it's not official until we tell Randall. He's been strangely quiet lately. I hope everything's okay."

Adam stepped into the living room which was his bedroom and dialed Randall's number.

"Greetings," Randall said. "Funny you should call just now. I have some news."

"So do I, but you go first."

"Drew is gone."

"Sweet! How'd you get rid of him?"

"I didn't have to. Like you said, there was nothing to worry about. He just announced his friends were ready to have him back and he would be heading over to the Mission."

"See? I told you it would be fine."

"He was really gracious about it, and bought me a bottle of organic wine and everything. I feel like a little bit of a jerk." Randall paused, then laughed. "But that's nothing compared to the huge sense of relief."

"You sound really happy."

"I am, but that's not the only thing. Here's the really trippy part. The next morning, I decided to celebrate having my place back to myself again with a little dawn patrol at the beach, so I got into the wetsuit and grabbed the board. The waves were sort of messy, but I hung in there and it was decent, considering. I had figured I'd stay out there just a few minutes longer when I took a little spin in the washing machine."

"That doesn't sound like fun."

"Luckily, it wasn't too bad and I got out of it still breathing air, mostly. I was a little beat up, though, and I crawled out to chill on the sand for a while before heading home. Now get this. As I was sitting on the beach spitting out seawater, this guy came walking along. He was wearing a classic beige and tan cabana set with long pants—super nice. He had great tortoise shell glasses. Leather sandals. He was an old guy but he looked like he could've stepped out of a Fellini movie."

"I've never seen a Fellini movie."

"Neither have I, but even so.... He asked if I was okay and sat down next to me. I warned him the sand was cold, but he said he didn't mind. He had seen what had happened and wanted to sit with me for a few minutes just to make sure I was all right. We talked for a while, and he asked me what I did. I told him about Hengist and my photography and my writing. And here's where it gets crazy." Randall paused for effect. "He told me his name was Sal, and said he was a writer himself. We talked about the City for a while and he told me about his heyday when he was in his twenties and thirties. We might have sat there for what could've been an hour or so, hard to say. Finally, he helped me to my feet and walked me and the board back to my apartment. I remember him smiling and talking for another minute or two, but I don't really remember letting myself in or getting out of the wetsuit. The next thing I knew, I was in bed, waking up after a heavy sleep. I'm pretty sure I had to have dreamt the whole thing, but the feeling is still hanging around. It was really vivid. And I definitely went down to the water that morning because the wetsuit was hanging in the bathroom and still damp."

"Wow, man. Whether you were awake or dreaming or outright hallucinating, I'd say you met your spirit guide."

"Yeah, y'know, I think I did." Randall was silent for a moment. "But you said you had some news too."

When Gustavo came home, the apartment was warm and filled with a wonderful aroma, though he knew dinner wasn't anything that took much effort. It was one of his and Jason's favorite shortcut meals: DIY pizza on a pre-baked, store-bought crust. They made canned tomato sauce better by sautéing a little fresh garlic first, which was the enticing fragrance greeting Gustavo when he opened the door. He had a bottle of red wine he'd picked up on the way. The oven was preheated. Jason was in the kitchen shredding mozzarella with a box grater.

"Hello there," Gustavo said, putting down the wine.

"Hello." Jason smiled and let himself be hugged gently without getting the food on Gustavo's clothes.

"So you got the job." Gustavo went to a drawer for the corkscrew.

"I got the job."

"Are you happy about that?"

"I think so?"

The new job paid a little better, and it was in the city, which was the goal. But it was for a bigger company, which seemed like a minus. And for all the firm's professed aspirations toward innovation, it was still no closer to what brought Jason to San Francisco.

Gustavo poured the wine and handed Jason a glass, then watched him grate cheese for a moment before saying, "Do you know what it is that you really want?"

Jason took a sip of wine. "I'm gonna show you something I've been doing." He washed his hands and went to their bedroom for his sketchpad. When he came back, he issued a disclaimer about how he wasn't very good.

Gustavo was surprised. He opened the pad at the kitchen table and looked at the drawings with obvious pleasure. Jason sat down too, but didn't watch as Gustavo turned over each page. Gustavo was quietly amazed. "I had no idea you were doing this. When did you start?"

"A few weeks ago. They're not much." Jason got up and went to the counter again.

"They're good. They're obviously beginner drawings, but there's life here." Gustavo pointed to a green sketch. "That one's totally me. You must've done these when I was sleeping. I had no idea you were so sneaky. But seriously, man—these are good. Don't put 'em down."

"I bought a book about how to draw. That helped a lot."

"So you want to be a visual artist?"

"I dunno. Maybe? Even if I have some kind of talent I never knew about, there's this thing I've been chasing since before I moved here. It's hard to explain, but it's alive. I want to be a part of that something. Most of the time, I feel like it's rushing past me. All those people who move here thinking it's about making money and spending it have nothing to do with that thing that's alive."

"Hey," said Gustavo as he put the pad on the table. He went over to Jason and held him close, not paying attention to any food spatters. "I know what that thing is."

24

In a downtown conference center and nearby park, a large annual environmental exposition was taking place. Visitors from all over Northern California and beyond had gathered to hear presentations from advocates, alternative resource groups, and companies focused on sustainability. At the tabling event in the lobby, Randall, wearing his customary white Oxford button-down, wandered through the crowd and browsed the various exhibitors.

Looking around the room, he noticed Oliver several tables away. Randall watched for a while, keeping a cautious distance. Oliver was talking with some people representing a rainforest-friendly agricultural project. He was looking very handsome, and suddenly more so when he broke into a smile. Randall was about to walk away when he got caught staring, so he put up a hand in greeting. Oliver waved back. He made no attempt to retreat, so Randall gradually made his way closer till they stood a few feet apart. Randall picked up a thick, brightly colored publication in front of him and held it near his nose with a noisy sniff.

"Mmm... ink stink. Every once in a while, you find one of

these brochures printed on really absorptive paper and the smell is," Randall sniffed again, "di-stink-tive."

Oliver, bemused but curious, said, "I think that sometimes happens with soy ink."

"But I wonder why it would," said Randall. "About a third of all of our newspapers have some amount of soybean oil in the ink. They started doing that in the '70s because of rising petroleum prices. So if soy's the reason, it seems like things should go wrong more often than they do. I can't figure out why every now and then, you run into a batch of printed material that smells like it was made from rancid rutabagas."

Oliver laughed. "Maybe it was and that's the problem. How's it going, Randall?"

"I can't complain. And yourself?"

"Doing okay."

"I'm glad to hear that. How do you like the expo?"

"It's pretty good this year. The turnout seems good, too. Actually, I'm starting to max out on all the faces. Would you like to go have lunch somewhere?"

"I'd be happy to. Do you like falafel? I know a pretty good place." As they made their way through the lobby doors to the corner, Randall said, "Or we could eat mushrooms. Did you hear the presentation by the fungus guy?"

"No. Was it good?"

"Check this out: many industrial contaminants can be broken down into harmless compounds by fungi. It's called mycoremediation. Theoretically, you could neutralize toxic waste with mushrooms, then throw them in a stir fry."

"Wow."

They decided on the falafel restaurant, and were mildly disappointed that it didn't offer mushrooms.

While they munched pita sandwiches, Randall said, "Are you still at Grateful Peas?"

Oliver shook his head. "I left when the semester started."

"Oh yeah, I meant to ask you how grad school is going. It must be really exciting."

"It's more fun than I expected. Some of it's confusing. The funding part is clunky, which I'd heard about."

Randall talked about his job search. He told the Drew story, which made Oliver laugh.

Then Oliver asked, "Are you dating anybody now?"

Randall smiled. "Not really. How about you?"

Later in the day, Oliver and Randall lay with the covers pulled up to their chins. The ocean chill was creeping into Randall's studio, and the light from the window was a matching grey. Randall risked extending an arm into the cold air to switch on a lamp.

"I missed the talk on Bay Area Wetlands," said Oliver.

"I'm sorry," said Randall.

"No, it's fine. I'm glad we did this instead."

"So am I. I really enjoyed it."

After a moment, Oliver said, "You haven't mentioned Adam."

"I wasn't sure if I was supposed to or not."

"It's okay. I don't mind if you talk about him."

"You miss him."

"Yeah. I think about him a lot."

"Maybe this is out of line, but I think you should give him a call."

Ted arrived on Russian Hill a little early, took a window table, and ordered a glass of Prosecco. In a little while, Peter showed up, handsome as ever, wearing a thick pullover. Ted waved him over.

"Great sweater."

"Thanks. I bought it in Ireland."

The server checked in with them, and Peter ordered a glass of the same wine. On the other side of the window, a couple stood near the door, studying the menu.

"How's work?" Peter asked with a look of concern.

"The term is underway. I'm teaching just two classes right now in addition to the other shit they've got me doing."

"On the phone, it sounded like things might be looking better?"

"I've decided to stop thinking about it."

"That's good, but are things sort of okay?"

"We've approached California Collegiate. Of course I want them to agree. It's unclear if they will, but then I realized I was too invested in a situation I couldn't have any more influence over than I already had, and I'd had enough. So I'm done with somehow trying to move mountains with my mind."

"That's great. I wish I knew how to do that," said Peter.

"In all honesty, I don't really know how to do it either. So how's Jerry doing?" Jerry was Peter's husband of the last nine years.

"He's fine. He leaves for a conference in Seattle next week. How's your mother?"

Ted's mother was fine. He was planning a visit for Thanksgiving. They talked about Ted's brother, niece, and nephew. They were living like good suburbanites.

Peter's wine came and they drank to old times. Outside, a cable car trundled by.

"It's exactly the same," said Ted, his gaze moving around the small dining room.

"Yeah, which is saying something. The City really doesn't look so hot."

"It's squalid," Ted said with more sorrow than anger.

They looked out of the window for signs of the apocalypse and drew some comfort, which they agreed was illusory, from the fact that the part of the world they could see at that instant still looked okay. It was still mostly there.

Peter said, "Do you remember when you first arrived and it was the most magical place you had ever been to in your life?"

"Yeah, that's what really kills me."

"It's still beautiful, though."

"Yeah, it's still beautiful."

The server came by again and they ordered dinner. Then Ted said, "There was something I was about to ask you, but I can't remember what it was. Oh well, it'll come to me."

Richard and Chuck said goodnight to the other four members of the League of Lavender Engineers. Chuck went into the kitchen to load the dessert plates in the dishwasher while Richard went through the living room to gather up glasses. It had been another lovely evening, though Mark seemed to have a had a little too much of that bitter digestif that made its way out at the end. Chuck liked collecting and showing off those interesting liqueurs, but they made the evening too boozy.

Everyone had admired the new rug. There seemed to be no question of getting a dog now, though Chuck had suggested that they could just hang it on a wall—the rug, not the dog. But all the walls were already full of art. Richard mentioned the possibility of taking down some of his photos, but Chuck wouldn't hear of that. Maybe they just needed a bigger house, Chuck joked. Richard said that they could get a bigger house for more art and more liqueurs and more bottles of wine, and the dog could even have an apartment of its own.

25

IT WAS A CLEAR, brilliantly blue late summer day, and the city was warming up. Adam and Randall stood on the sidewalk with their backs to Stern Grove. In front of them was a long, white neoclassical rectangle with decorations glazed in turquoise, bright blue, and jade green that might have graced a temple of Neptune. Surrounding it was a perfectly mown lawn.

"What is it?" Adam asked.

"It's the Central Pump Station for the Merced Manor Reservoir, which is the large structure just behind it."

"It's glorious."

"I thought you might dig this."

"Those crazy dolphins or whatever they are with the tridents are really something."

"I think they're guarding the place."

Randall followed Adam up to the column-framed entrance, obviously closed to the public. A stylized cascade the color of a swimming pool hung above the door, frozen in mid-fall.

Adam surveyed the building in mute fascination.

"We should look at the reservoir too. It's less exciting but the staircase to the top is pretty good," Randall said.

They went back to the sidewalk and around the corner, checking out the infrastructure between the pumping station and the larger mass of concrete that held the water, then went over to the multilevel, terraced staircase that led to the roof of the reservoir.

"This is a helluva thing too," said Adam. They ascended the steps and walked the edge, taking in the panorama of southwestern San Francisco and Daly City.

While they were looking out at the sky over the Pacific, Randall said in a guilty sounding voice, "I have a confession to make."

"Oh yeah?"

"Yeah, well, I don't know how you're gonna feel about this, but I really should tell you."

"C'mon, just tell me."

"I hooked up with Oliver."

It caught Adam by surprise, but then he said, "Well, so what?"

"Does it bother you at all?"

"No, it doesn't."

"You're thinking about it, though."

"Well, I didn't see it coming, but it's okay. It's just that I've been wondering if I should call him. It would be weird not to tell him I've decided to stay, but I don't wanna make a big deal of it. He—" Adam frowned. "He shouldn't think I decided because of him, but I'm not sure how to say that in the right way. But yes, I would like to see him."

"I have another confession. I suggested he call you. I didn't mention you've decided to live here, but I did tell him to call you. Sorry if I overstepped my bounds."

"No, you didn't. It's totally okay. Just curious—who mentioned my name first?"

"He asked how you were."

"Anything else?"

"He misses you."

"He said that?"

"I told him to call you. Obviously, he hasn't."

"Interesting." Adam was silent for a moment.

"But you're not mad we hooked up?"

"Nah. Hook up with whoever you want. It's none of my business, and it's not like I've seen a lot of him lately anyway."

When they reached the staircase again, Adam said, "This place is awesome. What should we do now?"

"How about a strip club?" Randall asked.

"Can that really be as much fun as the Central Pump Station?"

"A different kind of fun."

Duane dialed Seth's number. It rang three times before Seth picked up.

"Oh hey, Duane. It's great to hear from you. How are you?"

"Pretty great, actually. Some amazing things have been happening. I was hoping you'd like to get together for a drink, and I can tell you all about it."

"I'd really love to, but I'm in the middle of packing and everything is really hectic right now. But I hope we can get together again before I leave."

"Leave? I don't think you mentioned going anywhere."

"I'm sorry. I meant to tell you. I'm moving to L.A."

"Wow, how exiting. Somehow, I didn't see that coming. But that sounds great."

"Yeah, well, I've really had it with San Francisco. It's like a completely different place now, and the art scene is in the toilet. I can't make as much money here anymore, so I'm going to L.A. Not that that's not a shitty place too, but it's a different kind of shitty, and I just need to get away from here. But I hope you'll come and visit."

"Yeah, sure. I'd be curious to see it."

"You should come check it out sometime."

"I'll definitely do that."

"And let's get together before I leave."

Eugene had just got out of the shower when his phone rang. He was going to have dinner with Steve and Hector and another friend of theirs, and they said they'd check in before they left to pick him up, but the call was from Cody.

"Hey, stranger," said Eugene, "I've been wondering how you've been."

"I'm okay. I'm in rehab."

There was a very slight pause before Eugene said, "But you're okay?"

"Yeah."

"I've missed you."

"I'm glad to hear that. I've missed you too. I'd like to see you."

Later that evening after he got home, Eugene said to Adam, "Sometimes I'm not too bright."

They were in Adam's room not watching the television, which was on but muted. Adam switched off the picture.

"Honestly, I don't think you could've been expected to figure it out."

"I still feel like a fool."

"Why? Just because there were some slightly sketchy things going down, and he stopped returning calls?"

"It makes sense now, but I figured he'd ghosted me."

"But he didn't really."

"Yeah, no he didn't." Eugene was still slightly stunned.

"He said he's okay?"

"Yes, but I don't really know what that means."

"What happens now?"

"I don't really know that either, though we're gonna have dinner this week," said Eugene. "I guess I'll find out."

26

JASON HAD BEEN in his new job for a few days and was starting to make himself as much at home as he knew how. He took a seat on a shaded bench in a public space between the office towers and pulled his sketchpad out of the bag next to him. From his seat, he had a good view of a bland but convenient piece of sculpture, and he started blocking it out in dark grey charcoal pencil. The air was slightly too warm for most people to be dressed for the office.

Richard came downstairs with the bag lunch he had packed. He noticed Jason sketching and chose a bench a little distance away. As Richard ate, he occasionally glanced over at him, careful not to stare. Jason's pretty, rosy-cheeked face was serious with concentration, but calm too. There was purpose and thoughtfulness. It was the lunch hour, yet there was no phone call, no text messaging, no gigantic iced drink, no distraction, no idleness.

When Richard finished his lunch, he stood up and walked over to where Jason was drawing.

"Hi there. Forgive me for interrupting you, but I saw what

you were doing, and it looked interesting. Do you often draw at lunchtime?"

Jason looked up and smiled. "It's a new thing. "I'm trying to find more time to draw."

"It seems like a good day for it."

"Yeah, the sun makes the shadows and highlights really dramatic."

"I know what you mean about the shadows. I'm a photographer. Mind if I sit down?"

"Please, go right ahead," Jason said. He worked silently for a moment. "Do you have trouble making time for your photography?"

"Yes and no. It's hard to remember to do the things I want to do sometimes, but I try to take a photo every day," said Richard. "You're right about the contrast on days like today, though I like to shoot when it's overcast too. I can see more detail on a cloudy day."

"Sometimes I like the foggy days best of all," Jason said.

"You must like San Francisco, then."

"Yeah, I do. It's the first place I've ever chosen to live."

"Me too," said Richard. That was mostly true. He had also chosen his university, a place that had offered him the kind of experiences he needed to make his way in the world. But he had chosen the City as home.

"How long have you lived here?" Jason asked.

"I think it's twenty-four years now."

"Wow. I only just moved here a little while ago. You must really love it."

Richard studied the sculpture Jason was drawing, then said, "Yes, I do."

Jason worked at the paper in front of him quietly for a little while, then looked up at the buildings. "Sometimes on days like today, I feel like if I look at everything more carefully, it means more of me is really here."

"Y'know," Richard said, smiling, "I think so too."

Across town, Ted had made his way out of the president's conference room and back to the MFA offices. Adam was away from his desk and Delma was sitting by herself.

"Did Adam just go down the hall or something?"

"Yeah, he should be back any minute. How'd it go?"

"Pretty well, considering. We can retain this building, and they have space for some of the programs at their Mid-Market campus. I'll tell you about it when we have more time. Anything happen while I was in there?"

"Not much. Ellen Russo dropped by."

"Oh crap!" Ted put a hand to his head. "I'm a terrible person. I just remembered something I was supposed to do. I have a phone call to make right away."

Down the hall, Adam had stepped into the lobby on his way back from the restroom. He took out his phone, scrolled to Oliver's number, and held his breath.

In Berkeley, a class Oliver was the teaching assistant for had just finished, and Oliver headed outside for a moment to check messages. He squinted in the sunlight and waved as another grad student in his program called to him on the way into the building. Oliver took his phone out of his pocket to check messages, and almost jumped when the phone buzzed that very instant.

Hello there.

Oliver smiled and typed *Hello there, yourself.*

That evening, Jason found more time for drawing. Gustavo was on the bed, this time not under the covers but reclining on one elbow in jeans and a t-shirt with bare feet.

"Should I do anything?"

"I think that's good. How long can you hold that pose?"

"I dunno. My right shoulder is okay for now, but I could see where it could start to hate me after a while."

"We'll make this one quick."

"I could take my clothes off. That would might make it even quicker."

"Maybe for the next pose."

Jason stuck the end of his tongue out of the corner of his mouth as he concentrated. Gustavo's feet were both a challenge and a pleasure to draw. The weather was getting warmer, and even in a San Francisco apartment that was usually a little chilly, posing naked wouldn't be uncomfortable.

It was an enticing evening. The September afternoon heat had peaked around three thirty, but the air was still very warm. When Eugene arrived for dinner on Valencia Street, Cody was already waiting outside the restaurant, smiling and wearing a polo shirt, handsome as ever.

"Hello," said Eugene.

"Hello. It's been a while," Cody said, still smiling, but with something like hesitation in his eyes. "Glad you could make it."

"Yeah, me too. Very nice to see you."

"You too."

They went in and sat down. The server asked if they wanted to get some drinks started. Cody ordered mineral water. Eugene ordered the same.

They spent some time staring at the menu.

"I have some concerts coming up," Cody said. The tone was conversational, but a little impersonal.

"That probably means you're leaving town, huh?" Eugene didn't hide his disappointment.

"There'll be a few trips, but some of the things will be local. I was invited by an East Bay ensemble to be the baritone soloist in Gabriella Simoni's new oratorio. That one'll premiere here at the Herbst and in Berkeley and Palo Alto in October."

"Am I allowed to come?"

Cody laughed. "Please come. It's by a living composer, and nobody's been told if they like it yet."

South of Market, the sidewalks were filled with people out having fun. Duane had told his roommates he was headed out to look for more bikers to photograph, but he became distracted by the weather and the mood of lightness in the air. Soon he found himself walking through the door of the same bar where he had met Perry that fateful night, and to Duane's amazement, Perry was there again, sleek and debonair as before, with the distinctive bright green cocktail in front of him.

"Hello there!" said Duane, sitting down.

"Hey! How's the biker project going?" Perry had remembered.

"Really great, as a matter of fact. And thank you for encouraging me. It was like everything just starting happening after that."

"I'm glad I could be of some help, but you're the one who made it happen."

"Even so, you...you were inspirational."

"Glad to hear it. So what happened?"

"As soon as I had a business card to hand out, I starting noticing all these great potential models. Through one of those guys, I got a part-time gig as an intern at a commercial portrait studio. That company is letting me use its facility in the Haight to work on my own portraits."

"That's fantastic! So are you thinking about becoming a professional photographer?"

Duane wavered for a second, then said with a confident smile, "Well, actually I'm considering floral design instead."

"Hey, it's all about following your nose!"

"That's what I think too," said Duane. "Excuse me, but is that a Grasshopper?"

"Yes, it is. I highly recommend them. They're delicious!"

Ted stopped by Lacey's a little before noon on a Saturday. Gustavo was talking to another customer but caught Ted's smile and smiled back. Ted went over and examined the poetry section, stopping when he found a certain slim volume by a local press. He carefully slid it free from its neighbors and turned the pages, stopping now and then to read. After a little while, he pushed it back to where he had found it. He browsed the recent fiction, finding a little collection of stories and essays by a Bay Area writer that looked entertaining. By then, Gustavo had finished his conversation and walked over to where Ted was standing.

"That's supposed to be really good," said Gustavo, seeing the book in Ted's hand.

"Nice. I could use something really good."

"Everything okay?"

"Yeah, just a tiring week, but I managed to put a big problem to bed. Administration is really the pits."

"Well, I hope you can forget about it for the weekend, at least."

"Yeah, it'll be a quiet couple of days in the house hiding from the world, though I plan to be at your open mic this week."

"Man, it would be so great if you could come."

"I should apologize again for not coming before. I've really wanted to."

"I understand. And I really hope you can get to this one, but if not, that's okay too."

"Well, I have to get to this one because my ex insists. He's going to be there with an old friend of his that Randall DeVries invited, and they told me I had to go too."

Ted said this with an amused expression. He bought his book, then went out into the street.

When Adam suggested he and Oliver get together for lunch in Berkeley, he didn't mention anything about his plans for the not-too-distant future. When he came walking up Shattuck, Oliver was standing outside the brewpub squinting in the sun, his hair shining in the light. His gaze met Adam's from a long way away.

As he arrived, Adam said, "Hey there, Mr. Oliver."

"Hey there."

They went inside and found a table. They made conversation about Adam's BART ride and Oliver's family, and the server came and took their order.

"Randall's got a job," said Adam. "It's a photo supply and rental shop in Emeryville. He likes it, but it's definitely less convenient."

They talked about Randall for a while. Oliver asked about Eugene.

Then Adam said, "I've decided to stay in San Francisco."

"I'm glad." Oliver was smiling.

"I wanted to tell you right away but didn't want you to feel pressured."

"I don't feel pressured."

"Good." Adam smiled. "It looks I'll have a job at CUE. Ted says he'll have to post it, but it's mine. Eugene and I are looking for an apartment. Anyway, I'm staying."

Their beers arrived. When the server had gone, Adam was still smiling but more serious.

"Hey, listen, there's something I need to say. I'd really like it if we dated, but I don't know if I... I mean, if you still wanted to go out with me, would it matter if we were... what I'm trying to say is would it be okay if we..."

"...were open?"

"Yeah. I know we talked about it, and I really like being with you, but I don't know if we want the same things."

"Well," said Oliver, "I had a good time with Randall. It seems like a shame not to do that again."

"That's great. I just, I dunno why it was such a big deal for me to say, but I'm glad it's okay because it's you I really like. I... this is wonderful. Anyway, I hope that doesn't mean you wanna go out with Randall and not with me."

Oliver shook his head and laughed. Adam laughed too but then became serious again.

"I guess it'll be a little tricky now that you're gonna be over here all the time because of school."

"I can go to San Francisco sometimes. And you can come over here sometimes."

"Yeah." Adam relaxed a little. "Dating."

"I promise you don't have to date my whole family too."

"Well, maybe they wouldn't mind having me over for dinner once in a while."

27

WEDNESDAY EVENING AT LACEY. Randall got a round of applause as he raised the mic a little and deadpanned, "So this one's called 'The Stripper with Chicken Knees.'"

Ken called up Larry and asked what he was doing for the weekend.

Larry said to him, "Saturday night, I'm gonna go out for dinner. And after that, I thought I'd go over to the All-Star Male Theater and check out the Stripper with Chicken Knees."

Ken didn't know what he was talking about. "How do you mean, 'Chicken Knees'?"

Larry told him, "You know, he's got knees like a chicken."

"Aw, c'mon. People don't have knees like chickens. I don't even know what a chicken's knees look like. Do chickens even have knees?"

"Of course they do. Everybody knows that. Otherwise, they'd have to goose-step. Anyway, I can't believe you've never heard of this guy. People come from all over to catch his act."

Ken couldn't believe it. "You're pulling my leg... chicken knees!"

"I'll tell you what, Ken, you have dinner with me Saturday, and then we'll go see this thing. Then we'll see if I'm kidding you."

So Saturday came along, and Ken met Larry for dinner at Joe's

*Restaurant and they had a nice time. Then they walked over to Jones
Street to the All-Star Male Theater. The headliner was Vince Dexter.*

*Larry told Ken, "That's the one! That's the Stripper with Chicken
Knees!"*

*He was going on at nine, and it was already a quarter to nine
when they decided to go in. They stood in line at the entrance with a
doorman and a velvet rope and everything. At the door, the manage-
ment had put up headshots of all the entertainers. And above them
all, a little larger than the rest, was a photo of Vince Dexter, a handsome blond fellow of about twenty-five.*

Ken was starting to half-believe it. "This I gotta see."

*So they paid their admission and sat close with a good view of
the stage. Ken had never been in there before. It was a very tasteful
theater of its kind, with new seats and striped wallpaper. Everybody
was very well-behaved.*

*Then over the sound system, they announced him. "The All-Star
Theater is proud to present Vince Dexter!" And they played a rock
and roll record, the very latest thing. Really hip stuff. And out onto
the stage came Vince, and you would have thought he was a movie
star. He was dressed in a pair of beige chinos and a casual but very
sharp short-sleeved shirt, just like a young executive on vacation.
Classy. As Vince Dexter danced to the music, he removed his clothes
very artistically.*

Ken said to Larry, "Hey, he really does have chicken knees!"

"See?" Larry told him.

"Well, I'll be a rubber chicken!"

*It was mind-blowing. Then Ken thought, I'll bet they're fake. But
then he tried to figure out how you would fake chicken knees. After a
while, he just had to accept those chicken knees were really chicken
knees, and that was all there was to it.*

*At the end of the evening, Ken told Larry, "You were absolutely
right. If I'd had a ten riding on it, I would've lost my money. That
man has chicken knees."*

Vince was handsome and had a great personality. But there was no question that what made the act was the chicken knees. Maybe he had other talents, but Vince was able to retire at thirty-five and purchase his first commercial real estate property on the strength of those wonderful chicken knees. As he got older, he remained a very attractive man. Occasionally, someone from the All-Star Theater days would recognize him and ask, "Say—aren't you the Stripper with Chicken Knees?" Vince would protest with a small wave of his hand and a self-deprecating smile. "You're so kind to remember."

At the end of the evening, Jason was exhausted as usual but catching a second wind as the afterparty started to gather. Randall was talking with a cute, hunky little dark-haired guy about Jason's own age. Three older men approached them, one of whom was wearing tortoise-shell glasses. Randall was making introductions and there were handshakes all around. He motioned for Gustavo to come over, and suddenly Gustavo was laughing and saying something to Randall in amazement. Gustavo and Randall saw Jason and waved him over.

"Ted, this is my boyfriend Jason. Jason, this is Ted whom I've talked about so many times. And I can't believe he's here with his friends Peter and Sal. I'm so honored that you all came tonight."

Randall introduced the other young guy to Jason as Adam. As they were all discussing where they should go for a drink, suddenly Orion was standing there with two boyfriends.

"Gustavo! That poem rocked!"

"Thanks, Orion. I think there were some real writers in the house tonight but thank you."

"So modest! Hey, you wanna come by my place? A couple of friends are coming over and we're gonna hang out and play some music."

"That sounds great, but I've been asked out by some friends of Randall's."

Orion looked at Randall for a moment, then back at Gustavo. "Okay, well, we'll miss you. Great poem!"

28

"WHAT ARE YOU WEARING?" Randall said lewdly into the telephone.

Adam and Eugene were standing in their new kitchen with a roll of off-white masking tape and many paint chips in unrelated colors.

"A bunny rabbit suit," said Adam.

"You know, some people are into to that kind of thing."

"Hey, that's exactly the reason I moved to this town."

"What are you up to this evening?"

"Eugene and I are trying to decide what colors to paint the place."

"Whaddya say I come over with Chinese food?"

"Sounds good, though we still don't have a table."

"Maybe we'll go out instead."

They agreed he'd come over in twenty minutes.

After ending the call with Randall, Adam said, "I love the quality of light in my room, but I want a color. Plain white feels like I gave up too easy." There was a deep blue that was interesting but would've been very dark. He held up a card with increasingly paler tints of lemon yellow.

"I dunno if yellow is right."

"One of the lighter ones would be good in here," said Eugene.

"Yeah, it would."

They taped the card to the kitchen wall.

The new place was another one bedroom, but adjacent to the kitchen was a dining room, which Eugene took for himself. Randall lent them a camping mattress and drove them over with their clothes. They moved in during a spell of very warm weather, and the thin cotton bedspread that had been Adam's door curtain was almost too much to sleep under.

Adam accepted the student services manager job.

Eugene applied to a doctor of physical therapy program.

Over the weekend, they bought a table. Randall gave them a yard sale chair.

Oliver came by with some red wine made by a friend in his program, and stayed overnight.

And on Monday morning, Adam walked to work.

ACKNOWLEDGMENTS

Thank you many times over to Jerry Wheeler for your fine editorial counsel. Heartfelt thanks to Burt Manaster for your fatherly fellowship while this book was brought into being. To Matt Miller, my gratitude for your encouragement when this project was just a few character sketches. And profound appreciation for the assistance of the people of the San Francisco Public Library, and the GLBT Historical Society Archive.

.

ABOUT THE AUTHOR

Rob Beck is a San Francisco Bay Area writer and illustrator for whom cities and their many lives hold unending fascination. This is his first novel.